ABOUT THE BOOK

When Bill Dan Alderdice befriended the old Dutchman, Jacob Walzer, on his deathbed, he had no idea that
the gesture would lead him on a treasure hunt for the old
Dutchman's hidden gold mine. The time was the early
1870's when hostile Apaches still occupied the Arizona
region. With five new friends including a fellow Texan,
a titled Englishman, a Mexican, and the attractive Letitia
Barry and her mother, Bill Dan leads an expedition up
the rugged, desolate slopes of Superstition Mountain,
which towers some 4,000 feet above the desert floor near
Phoenix, Arizona, in search of the mine. With few clues
to help them, this group of six disparate people becomes
one cohesive family, sharing the natural wonders of life
in the open terrain and the frustrations of their quest.

MYSTERY
OF
SUPERSTITION
MOUNTAIN

BY
OREN ARNOLD

Illustrated by Jimmie Ihms

Harvey House, Inc.
Publishers
Irvington-on-Hudson, N. Y. 10533

Dedicated
with love
to another valiant heroine adventuring in Arizona,
my daughter
JUDY

Library of Congress Catalog Card Number 76-185060.
Manufactured in the United States of America.
ISBN 0-8178-4871-1, Trade Edition.
ISBN 0-8178-4872-X, Library Edition.

Harvey House, Inc. Publishers
Irvington, New York 10533

Contents

Other Books by the Author

Arizona Under the Sun

Cowboy in Europe

Ghost Gold

Hidden Treasure in the Wild West

Irons in the Fire

Rancho M'Lee

The Story of Cattle Ranching

Young People's Arizona

Author's Note

This story is based on North America's most famous gold legend. Research for it began in 1927, when my wife and I first went to Phoenix and saw the sun rise over the red and purple majesty of Superstition Mountain. Within five years' time we had seen and photographed the nuggets which the Old Dutchman had given to the young man who visited him on his deathbed — the young man who is the hero of this story. A factual story of the Lost Dutchman's Mine is told in my book entitled Ghost Gold.

I am grateful to the countless librarians, research specialists, naturalists, old-timers and outdoorsmen who have helped me in explorations and on-the-scene studies. These include members of The Dons, a group distinguished as specialists in regional history and folklore. I am especially grateful to old and cherished friends, E. Osborn Foster and Arthur H. Weber, men with generous hearts and a vast knowledge of the wilderness.

O. A.

1

Meeting Under Gunfire

The tall young man riding west from Texas had learned long before never to top a rise in the earth without caution, without screening himself, and without studying what lay ahead.

At the moment, his nerve antennae seemed to be vibrating faster than usual. Without analyzing the cause, he dismounted, tethered his horse, and crept on his belly to the rim. For the remainder of his life he was glad that he did, for in the valley ahead lay a wagon and a handful of travelers who were being besieged by a band of Indians on horseback.

In the thin, clear air distances were deceptive, but the Texan guessed that the people were less than a mile away. A breeze was at his back and he could not hear rifle fire, but he could see spurts of smoke. His trained eyes squinted as he studied the scene intently.

"Four — no, five," he murmered to the grass and gravel which almost surrounded his face. "One of them's a woman. Only six Indians."

The defenders seemed to be firing slowly, no doubt to conserve their ammunition. The Indians circled at a trot out of easy rifle range, nagging the group and biding their time. The young man could detect no sign of any other Indians. Apparently a wandering band of marauders had come onto what they considered an easy prize.

"All right!" he whispered tight-lipped, as he backed away. He had already experienced his own terror of the wilderness more than once; first with Comanches in west Texas, then with the Mescaleros in New Mexico. These Indians were likely those that an Army major had told him to expect — Apaches, the fiercest of all tribes.

Still screened from the foray, he ran afoot about two hundred yards northward across the semidesert, dodging cactus and other thorny plants. The air seemed to crackle with late September dryness, so he had no trouble snatching armloads of knee-high grass burned tan and crisp by the sunshine. He piled the grass near the rim, then gathered deadwood from water-starved trees and shrubs nearby and added this to the grass. From a pocket he extracted one of his treasures — a small tin box, containing his fourteen remaining sulphur matches. One of these sufficed to set the grass ablaze.

He ran fast, got back to his horse, leaped on, and spurred. He swung southward a quarter mile, skirted boulders bigger than houses and weaved through a dense

growth of hard two-inch needles which pointed at him in stern warning. He kept the horse and himself well-screened from the battle, yet he continued to circle toward it.

Thus he came onto the little valley in a direction almost opposite the fire on the rim. He saw that his ruse had worked; the Indians had discovered his smoke, had paused in surprise and anxiety. Smoke in the northeast? No Indian would build a fire under such conditions.

Now the Texan took careful aim with his rifle and fired. His bullet went true. An Indian slumped over his own horse, clung there for a moment, then plunged to the ground. Three members of the besieged party ran out from the circle and shot at the fleeing Apaches, meanwhile shouting defiance. In another moment the young man had approached the wagon.

"Are you all right?" he asked. "Anybody hurt?"

"Not yet," a woman answered in a clear voice that showed no fright. "But if you hadn't come, mister. . . . Got any extra cartridges? We need. . . ."

"Just four of you?" he interrupted. He twisted in his saddle because his horse was restless from excitement, but he kept a tight rein on it.

"Yes."

"I thought I counted five. Well, I think we've buffaloed them. That fire — I set it — to worry them, to make them wonder. But we've got five now." He looked at the others of the group who were returning. "Hey, that one's not a man, either!"

"She's my mother." The person wore men's clothes and a man's hat.

The Texan swung down and stood spread-legged. He stared. "And one is black. A Negro," he said.

"That's Roxie Webb," the girl answered.

"Have to thank you, mister," the woman spoke out heartily as she approached. Her face showed deep strain, yet it glowed with pleasure. "We're beholden."

"No such, ma'am." Unconsciously the young man took off his hat. "You'd have done as much for me. Who are you? I haven't seen any white people in nearly three weeks. I guess you're heading west as I was — as I am."

The four nodded, but still held their rifles across their chests. At the same time they glanced sharply back toward the direction in which the Indians had fled. The young man felt the friendliness, but he also sensed the fear they had experienced. Yet they did not cringe nor complain. If need be, they would die with dignity, he well knew, because he had known their kind and had seen their courage.

He dropped his rifle into his saddle scabbard, then swung down, holding the reins for a moment before dropping them. His horse had settled now and remained quiet.

After a few seconds of mutual, silent appraisal, the girl answered him. "Mother, here, is Mrs. John Barry."

The woman was no taller than her daughter, he noticed, and in spite of the man's shirt and pants which she wore, she looked feminine and youthful. In a quick study of both women, he liked the directness of their eyes and especially the firm set of their lips.

"Ma'am," he acknowledged seriously, as he squeezed his hat with his big hand.

13

Both women were only chin-high to him, and because they were women, and because he had been on a long, lonely journey, he felt a homesickness surge up in him.

"We're from down South," the girl added, "so most people call mother Miss Nannie."

"Miss Nannie, ma'am." He felt more homesick than ever now. He became aware that the girl was studying him, and when he turned to her, he caught the rich violet of her eyes, which had seemed at first glance to be black. Her hair plunged below her shoulders in a black mass. He would have described her dress as the color of a wasp's nest. It had faded to a pale grey from much exposure, yet it was reasonably clean. Her voice was the feature that arrested him most. It was clear, yet muted, and it held a lyric quality.

As soon as he realized that he was staring, he turned away and faced the others. A young man stepped from the group and smiled — a young Mexican with perfectly aligned white teeth, skin the color of pecans, and a black mustache whose points seemed to be at least four inches apart. His smile was warm and friendly. He bowed slightly and addressed the tall Texan, "*Señor,* is *muchas gracias.* Is safe lifes. Me, everything mine now she is yours. Forever. *Amigo mio.*" He shifted his rifle to his left hand, so that he could extend his right hand.

"That's right," the fourth member of the party, the Negro, spoke for the first time. "Me too, sir," he said nodding emphatically. "If you hadn't come — man, man!"

He, too, was handsome, although his hair needed cutting and his face, which glistened with sweat, needed shaving. His clothing, like his companion's, was neutral in color, although he wore somewhat better boots than the Mexican. His old felt hat was cupped up jauntily in front. He smiled and said, "Roxie Webb is my name."

That remark prompted the Mexican to tell his name: "I, *señor,* am Leonti Tafoya de la Hernandez de la Herrera y Verlarde y Soto. At your service, *señor.*" He bowed a second time.

The girl hastened to explain: "Leonti risked his life to help us, mister, just as you did, and just as Roxie Webb did. I suppose we are all in the same boat, come to that. My name is Letitia Barry. People call me Tisha, or Tish."

"Ma'am," he acknowledged once more, but that was all he could say, and he wished he were more adept at conversation.

"We should say that we were wiped out," she resumed, speaking softly and looking far off, "back there, west of El Paso. Our train had twelve wagons and over thirty people. First it got split up in a cyclone and most were killed. Then, what with the rains and the Comanches and all. . . . If it hadn't been for Roxie, mother and I. . . . Well, you likely know what happens to women that the Indians capture."

"I've heard," the Texan murmured grimly.

"Once Roxie even buried us in sand, with only our noses out, so that he could lure the Comanches away. Then he sneaked back to help us. It was two days later that we picked up Leonti. This wagon and the team are his."

The tall boy swallowed. He understood thoroughly and nodded as he said, "Been through much the same myself."

Then the Mexican spoke. "Me, I was on the leetle reever, washing *el oro* — the gold — with the pans. *Sabé usted, señor?*" It was almost a pleading. "That flood the *señora* tell — he take my friend, our camp, everything but wagon and horses tied up the hills, some things in wagon. I find thees peoples, we stick together."

His was a story of tragedy, and the strain of it was reflected on the entire group. The newcomer suddenly realized that he was looking down at the others, due to his height of six feet, two inches. His bones and muscles were in proportion to his height; shoulders bulged through a faded, sweat-strained shirt; honey-colored hair spilled over ears and collar; restless black eyes bespoke the disquiet of oncoming manhood.

"Guess we all owe thanks to be alive," he murmured. "Strangers, far from anywhere, thrown together in this wild land, but still alive."

He had summed up the situation well. The four nodded — Mrs. Barry, her daughter, Letitia, the dark Roxie who seemed to be the newcomer's own age, and the equally youngish-looking Mexican with the ponderous name.

"You want to say your name?" the girl prodded.

The Texan felt himself blush. "Name of Allerdice," he managed, forcing a shy smile. "William Daniel. People — uh — mostly just call me Bill Dan." The name came out a soft Texas drawl.

The mother nodded pleasantly. "That's a right good name, son. Proud to know you, Bill Dan. Had two boys of my own . . . a good husband, too . . . until a big dust wind and a flood, then the Comanches. . . ."

"Mother! You promised to lay all that behind us!"

"Yes, dear, It's just that . . . well, Bill Dan would be close to Walter's age, and. . . ."

"I'm coming up twenty, ma'am," Bill Dan supplied softly, gently.

So, he reflected, here was a saddened mother with three refugees in her charge. No, four refugees now, if he included himself. Then somewhat to his own consternation, Bill Dan Allerdice realized that he could not be included as one of her charges. On the contrary, all four of these harassed and unhappy people whom he had rescued, were instinctively looking to him for leadership. The thought appalled him and was verified the next moment.

"What ought we to do now, Bill Dan?" the girl asked, her eyes wide as she waited for an answer.

With his hands in hip pockets, he turned toward the western horizon as if he were studying it. His face showed not a sternness but a rocklike quality. He spoke slowly. "Not much choice, I'd say. Best thing is to take stock of what we've got left, all of us together, then start off again. You folks get the wagon set up and ready. I'm going out to that Apache lying yonder."

"You aim to bury him?" Mrs. Barry asked.

"Won't have time. And it wouldn't be safe. They'll come to get him."

He rode to the corpse that lay sprawled on the desert gravel. It hurt him to see that the Indian boy was younger than he was. It gave him no satisfaction to remove a heavy leather pouch and a crude, lethal-looking knife, plainly a white man's hunting tool. Bill Dan didn't doubt that the real owner had lost his scalp, so he worked grimly, knowing the laws of survival. The pouch was about the size of a gallon bucket, though flatter in shape. He didn't take time to open it, but he figured that it held food.

Half an hour later the five refugees moved again toward the waning sun. They had enough food to maintain them, crude though it was. They had one cask full of water and another one partly full. All of them wore usable boots or shoes and clothing sufficient, at least, for the mild temperatures.

"Come bedtime," the mother said from her wagon seat, "I aim to thank the good Lord for sending you to us, Bill Dan."

"Yes," her daughter nodded agreement. "Yes, do."

"Ma'am, just thank Him for getting us together and keeping us alive. And maybe ask Him if He minds helping us on to some town."

Four hours later, they prayed together under a starlit sky.

Four days later, their prayers were answered.

The forlorn little party, subsisting now on the meat of jackrabbit and quail, plus a strange-looking gummy substance that Bill Dan had found in the dead Indian's pack, was in good physical shape, but low in spirits. That gummy stuff, Leonti Soto explained, was a *dulce* — a sweet — a candy-like food made by cooking the fat leaves of the mescal, a fantastic flower which grew as tall as thirty feet on the hillsides. The Indians, and also the Mexican people, Leonti said, considered this food very nourishing. These travelers also found it was tasty.

Although the party progressed generally in a westerly direction, Bill Dan knew that each one had the same unspoken goal — a goal that had already lured thousands westward.

He suggested that they find an Army outpost or a town somewhere, secure work to recoup their supplies, and rest themselves and their horses before pushing on to the California gold fields. One morning when he was making an inventory of their needs, he saw an early fog lift and reveal what Letitia Barry called "a sight to behold."

"It is that," Bill Dan agreed, and all of them paused to study the landscape.

Ahead was a mountain different in shape from any they had so far encountered. It seemed to be five or six miles away. "Maybe ten, the way this country can fool you," Roxie Webb said. It was not a single, cone-point peak, but a vast, flat, yet irregular tableland, with much deep sculpturing. From the center of this cloud-high wilderness, the nose of a rounded rock reached for the sky.

"It looks just like a weaver's needle," Miss Nannie Barry exclaimed. "Look at it, dear."

Her daughter said she had seen old women back in their home town of Henderson, Texas, making use of a shape such as this in their weaving. Leonti Soto merely laughed.

"She is *el sombrero, amigas* — the hat," he told them. "Look."

Leonti took off his wide-brimmed Mexican hat to show them the shape. With his hands he traced the graceful curves of the hat crown, then repeated the curves, pointing his hands to the landscape. "Is the same. Is maybe 'The Hat Mountain,' you think?"

The resemblance of a mountain peak to a hat made them smile, and the moment of whimsy seemed to rest their spirits. By this time the sun had thrown fantastic shades of light onto the mountain. Cliff faces that pointed straight up for two thousand feet glowed with crimson and gold, while in canyons purple mists hovered.

"I think it's a mystery mountain," Letitia Barry said. "It is so beautiful; maybe it is a good omen."

Somewhat reluctantly, the five moved on. Within ten hours they experienced a new moment of excitement: they came abruptly to a road which showed wagon ruts! Bill Dan told himself that he would never have guessed that such a simple, homely promise could stir him so deeply.

Scouting eagerly next day, they looked down onto fields of corn, cane, cotton, and pastures of cattle and sheep. Best of all, they could see houses in the haze not far from a silvery thread which, no doubt, was a stream.

"I guess we have made it into the Territory of Arizona," Bill Dan told his weary friends. "I talked with an Army major back at El Paso. He had been on duty over in this country. From what he said, I figure this must be the town of Tucson."

This conversation took place soon after breakfast, but it was sundown before they actually entered the town, which was about forty miles from the mountain. Hat

20

Mountain, they had named it. To their hungry eyes the town was a great city, although Bill Dan told them that it couldn't actually be a settlement of more than a few hundred souls.

It was not Tucson, they learned later.

When they finally rode up to the town's main street, they saw men sitting and standing around what seemed to be a small town hall of unpainted wood. They pulled up in front of the building.

People stared at them, but Bill Dan understood their natural shyness because he felt the same shyness in himself. Finally, one man rose from his chair and stepped down off the plank porch. He was well-dressed and clean, and had a jaunty-looking mustache and sideburns. There was an open friendliness in his eyes.

"Greetings!" he called, as he smiled a welcome.

Greetings? Bill Dan Allerdice reflected that that wasn't a word he would have used. Maybe howdy, hello, good evening — any of those. The man spoke in a voice that did not sound like country talk. The five of them could only stare at him.

"A hearty welcome, friends," the gentleman said. "You appear to have come quite a distance, and no doubt you are tired and hungry. So please alight; take your ease. Some of us will care for your animals, and we'll see that you are made to feel at home."

What he had said sounded good; almost enough to choke a body up, Bill Dan mused, as he glanced at Letitia Barry, who had already appeared at his side as he swung down from his horse.

"Who's he? He's not like the others," she murmured.

The gentleman spoke again, "Please feel at ease. All of us have been travelers in our time. And I know I don't look it or act it, but I belong here, too. It just happens that I am what they call an English remittance man. My former home was in Peterborough, Northants, England, but my home is here now. My name is Darrell Duppa. The people here have nicknamed me 'Lord Duppa,' because I am English." He laughed, and his laugh seemed to break the shyness of the townsfolk, for there was a stirring and some even came forward to shake hands.

Bill Dan smiled at them, then asked, "Is this Tucson, sir? Arizona Territory?"

"Arizona, yes. Tucson, no. Tucson is old and is a hundred and twenty-odd miles south. This town is new and is named Phoenix."

"Phoenix, sir?" That seemed like an odd word.

"Right. The name comes from the Phoenix bird in ancient mythology. It was destroyed in a fire, then rose from its own ashes, brighter, stronger, more beautiful than ever. Our town, now, is on the site of a prehistoric Indian civilization, the mound builders."

"Sir?" Bill Dan's brow had furrowed and he sort of smiled. Mrs. Barry, Leonti Soto, and Roxie Webb meanwhile stood near.

Lord Duppa laughed gently and some of the townsfolk joined in the laughter. "I will have to explain that," he said. "You see, the ancient people here were farmers just as we. . . ."

He did not finish. At that moment, two quick pistol

shots rang out on the street, fifty yards or so away. On top of the shots came a man's voice shouting: *"Eee-ea-A-A-A HOO-O-O- OOOOO! I'm a two-legged hellion from back in th' hills, and I'll shoot anybody who says I ain't!"*

Automatically, Bill Dan Allerdice swung his left arm to push Letitia Barry behind him, while in the same split second his right hand unholstered his own pistol.

He did not fire the pistol; he did not need to. As he looked up the street, he saw a shabby old man with a gray beard, whose white hair fell well down over his ears, wobbling and shooting his two guns at the evening sky. Obviously, he was thoroughly intoxicated and had just come out of a building that no doubt was the town saloon.

"I GOT ME A GOLD MINE WITH MILLION DOLLARS IN IT!" the old man bellowed to the hundred or so spectators. "GONNA BUY EVERYTHING IN THIS TOWN!"

Whereupon, he emptied his pistols at the stars.

2

Old Snowbeard the Dutchman

An old man, evidently a desert rat blowing off steam, is not to be taken too seriously, William Daniel Allerdice tried to tell the weary travelers. "Don't be afraid," he counseled. "I'm sure he's had too much liquor and is shooting off his mouth along with his guns. Anyhow — look. Somebody has taken charge of him — the sheriff, likely."

The moment of excitement was enough to cause him and Roxie, Leonti and Lord Duppa to start walking up the street.

"That's old Jacob Walz," Lord Duppa said. "A prospector. Everybody around here knows him. He lives in a shack near the river. A Negro woman does his cooking."

Roxie Webb's face lighted up. "A black woman? Like me? You're not joking?"

The others laughed gently. "Like you, Mr. Webb,"

25

Lord Duppa nodded. "But old enough to be your mother, I'm afraid."

"Are there other Negro people here?" Roxie asked in his Texas brogue. He had been born and reared near Houston.

"A few families, yes. Come to think of it, some young people, too. Close to your age, I should think. You are not twenty yet, I take it?"

Roxie grinned happily. "Not even eighteen. But I can whip boys and a lot of men older'n me. I mean, if I have to. I don't go around fighting. I just got muscles."

They reached the crowd of men standing at the village saloon. Bill Dan, conscious of their stirring, caught something of the undefined excitement when he heard a strong male voice coming from the saloon.

"No, I tell you," it said. "He isn't lying. He swears he's got gold, and he brought some to prove it!"

"A bag of dust, hey?" somebody asked. Bill Dan could see the intense interest in the faces of the bystanders.

"No, not dust." He watched as the man, who appeared to be the saloonkeeper, called out, "Come on in here, and I'll show you."

Lord Duppa commanded respect, so the four newcomers were able to get close to the man inside. Bill Dan watched the man open a small iron safe and lift out a pouch about eight inches long, which was closed by a drawstring. Dramatically, the saloonkeeper upended the pouch on the shiny top of the bar. A double handful of golden nuggets fell out.

"Whew-w-w-w!" Roxie Webb exhaled, expressing

the feelings of the others. Bill Dan stretched to his full height, the better to peer over Roxie's shoulder.

"This here is Old Snowbeard's gold," declared the barkeeper, who seemed now to feel his importance. "Left it here for me to keep safe, and I aim to do just that. I shoot mighty straight and fast when I have to. Isn't that right, men?"

A murmur of agreement could be heard in the room. Bill Dan decided that the barkeeper must be a man of position in Phoenix. It took half an hour to get all the facts, all the speculations. During that interval, he forgot about Mrs. Barry and Letitia, who were in their wagon, because here was something more than town fellowship for which he had hungered; here, he reflected, were drama and promise and hope.

Old Snowbeard the Dutchman, whose real name was Jacob Walz, had been living in Phoenix for six months and had made frequent trips into the surrounding hills to search for minerals. Arizona Territory was known to have many deposits of silver, copper, and other metals, including gold. Finding those deposits, of course, was enough to intrigue anybody. But most of the people in Phoenix were farmers, and traipsing off after ghost gold seemed questionable. On the other hand, a pile of shining nuggets. . . .

"It's what I was heading into California for," Bill Dan later said to the womenfolk who had been waiting in the wagon, none too patiently. "Gold!"

"*Seguro si, yo tambien.*" Leonti Soto often lapsed into Spanish when he was intent on something. "*Pero mucho oro aqui. ¿No es verdad?"* He looked questioningly at his friends, and they looked back at him in the same way.

"I understand you, *señor,* but I doubt whether your friends do," Lord Duppa said.

"Is sorry," Leonti smiled in quick apology. "Me, I forget, and. . . ."

"But you also speak English, I observe."

"Si, *señor,* I speak him perfect. Only, I forget to use him. I get excited. Is — how you say — yes, we go for California, the *oro* there, the gold, but maybe is *mucho aqui.* . . ."

Lord Duppa smilingly came to his rescue. "Much gold here."

"¡Si, si, gracias, amigo!" Leonti smiled back.

"California had a big rush in the 1850's, right enough," the Englishman reminded them. "Somebody found gold at Sutter's Mill. But that was over twenty years ago, and the best claims are all taken, most likely. Arizona, on the other hand, is still a virgin territory. If the old Dutchman has made a gold strike here. . . ."

The ideas provided food to meditate on as the five trail-weary newcomers settled down in the town. Every one of them agreed that Phoenix was a godsend. Here they could rest and the men could get work. The women could repair clothes and shoes and get ready to push on toward California later. It never occurred to any of the party that they might separate again, and Bill Dan as much said so to Letitia after supper that evening.

She agreed. "It's as if we were one family now. I guess

what we went through brought us close in spirit. Besides, none of us has any other kin out here. We have to help each other."

"Yes, ma'am," Roxie Webb nodded emphatically, for he and the other three were listening. Plainly, all of them felt a deep kinship and need for one another.

Mrs. Barry spoke. "I count myself lucky, me and Letitia. We will forever be beholden, first to Rox here, then to Leonti, and next to Bill Dan, for the way you saved our skins and helped us. I hope we can be a sort of family."

"I will say this, too," she added. "I am dog-tired, trail-tired. Tisha and Roxie are the only ones I have left. But if Leonti and Bill Dan want to stick with us, making it as if I had four big children, why I'll do what I can. I guess you, Bill Dan, will have to be the — well, the father, so to speak."

Everyone laughed at that suggestion, but Bill Dan felt self-conscious, even though he appreciated their trust in him.

"I mean it," Mrs. Barry went on. "If ever there is a final decision to be made about anything, I vote that Bill Dan should be the one to make it."

"Yes, ma'am," Roxie responded and Letitia nodded. Leonti Soto said, *"Seguro si,"* which means yes, indeed.

Whether he liked it or not, Bill Dan had acquired "people." The thought pleased him and at the same time sobered him. He didn't feel so old nor so mature as he knew he appeared; yet he welcomed the companionship which fate had sent him.

As he meditated on the idea, he found himself staring

covertly at Letitia Barry. The dancing flames from the campfire had highlighted her face with crimson. She looked so desirable! But Bill Dan warned himself sternly that he had no personal claim on her. Furthermore, Soto saw her first. Leonti was not only handsome and young, but he showed women every courtesy and had the quality that women call romance.

He suddenly rose from the fire and ambled over to curry his horse, Sam, which he had named for Sam Houston, the first president of the Republic of Texas. "Ho-o-o, boy," he greeted Sam, slapping him gently on the flank, but still thinking of Letitia Barry. "Need rubbing down; you've been wallowing in too much dirt, you old hammer-headed son of Satan."

Sam responded by butting Bill Dan in the side with his nose, then nipping him playfully on the arm. The intimacy and trust between man and horse stemmed from their long weeks together on the trail.

By the end of the first week in Phoenix, the "family" had repaired and moved into an abandoned four-room house constructed of sun-baked adobe bricks.

Lord Duppa explained about adobe bricks. "You see, we get only six or seven inches of rain here in a year, so the adobe bricks do not get melted down. The house could stand for fifty years in this arid country."

"Why, that's not enough rain to grow crops," Letitia pointed out.

"No, it isn't. So we irrigate. We get water from the Salt River. Matter of fact, it was a bride from Arkansas,

31

a girl just your age, who stopped here by the river one day, and never did go on to California. Both she and her husband helped a man named Jack Swilling to build a canal, and soon they had a fine farm. Her name was Mrs. Adaline Gray. You folks must meet her, because she really founded the town of Phoenix."

The most repairs that had to be made to their dwelling were to the roof and windows, and these were easy to do because several men of the town drifted in to help in a spirit of neighborliness. The town women brought in food, and so Mrs. Barry was able to develop a new and happy fellowship.

While the house was being repaired, Bill Dan found work with good pay as a teamster for a grocer who brought in supplies from Tucson. Because the trail between Tucson and Phoenix was dangerous, Leonti Soto rode with Bill Dan as a paid shotgun guard.

"Most of that territory is peaceful because only the Maricopa and Papago Indians live there," the grocer explained. "But bands of Apaches can drift down from the hills, and there have also been some white bandits. Don't ask questions if you are attacked; just shoot to kill."

Since there was no occasion when shooting became necessary, Bill Dan and Leonti were able to strengthen their friendship, each one teaching the other many things during the long hours of the ride together. Neither man ever mentioned Letitia Barry; both men seemed to sense that she was not a subject for discussion. Bill Dan did develop a brotherly love for this colorful son of old Mexico, just as he had developed a respect and affection for Roxie from his own East Texas homeland.

Roxie soon secured a job as horse wrangler, blacksmith, and an expert with livestock. He was adept at shoeing a mule, castrating a bull, or building a fence. He could laugh with gusto and sing beautifully, so he soon became popular with the people of Phoenix.

He also became popular with a Negro girl named Ellen Austin. She was not quite sixteen, but she possessed the capabilities of a frontier woman. Ellen had other admirers, Roxie soon discovered. At least four fellows had already staked claims to Ellen, but one by one in rip-roaring fistfights, Roxie eliminated them.

One night Bill Dan upbraided him for so much fighting; then he apologized when Roxie asked if he wouldn't fight for a woman he loved.

"Guess I would, Rox," Bill Dan replied, "but I'd try to win her without bloodshed."

During the interlude of settling down, working at new jobs, and resting their spirits from the hardships of the trail, the little family often mentioned Old Snowbeard the Dutchman. Bill Dan realized that when the old man showed the gold nuggets, he had stirred an attitude of greed in a number of the townfolk. Several groups had started to search for the gold, but some of them had not returned. It was rumored that they had been murdered.

But there was no concerted "gold rush." The people did not know where to rush to, for one thing, and besides, Jacob Walz was close-mouthed. When he was sober, he had little or nothing to say. In fact, he did not even hang around the saloons or the stores very much. It was when he was intoxicated that he spoke freely.

34

Leonti Soto discovered that he could buy a guitar in Phoenix, so, often after nightfall he entertained the people on Montezuma Street with impromptu songs. Even though he was a professed Roman Catholic, he attended a thatched house of worship erected by the Presbyterians, called the Brush Church. There he played his guitar as accompaniment for the hymn sings. Voluntarily, the people paid Leonti for these services, but he gave all the money that he earned to Mrs. Barry to keep for him, as did Roxie and Bill Dan also. She put all the money in glass jars and buried the jars after dark under the posts around their horse corral. She and Letitia were the only ones who knew under which posts the jars were hidden. The boys didn't want to know, they told her, because they might be tempted to spend the money foolishly. They preferred to pool it until the family had a sizeable stake. When Bill Dan gave up his hauling job to help the grocer build a bigger store in town, Leonti was put in charge of the owner's new meat market because he had had experience as a butcher. It was not too long before the strange migrant "family" from back east began to fit into the new oasis on the desert, and time slipped by quickly for all of them.

One night Bill Dan came home and said, "You know what? It is well into November. Some of the people in town are getting ready to celebrate Thanksgiving, and we ought to celebrate it, too."

"We need a calendar or an almanac," Mrs. Barry said. "Being busy this way, we can hardly keep track of the days." But frontier Phoenix had few such luxuries as calendars. Bill Dan, however, learned the date of Thanksgiving from a squad of United States Cavalrymen who rode through town on official business.

Soon after Thanksgiving, Mrs. Barry made another report to her family. "We have enough money for now," she said. "When you boys figure you are ready, we can start to outfit ourselves to hunt for that California gold."

"Moth-er!" Letitia almost screeched in protest, "and leave Phoenix? I've made friends here. They even want me to teach school."

"Don't doubt you have, dear. But we started for California, and so did the boys. People do say, though, that Mr. Walz has been in town twice recently with a pouchful of nuggets. Men have been trying to trail him to his mine, but I hear tell they have had bad luck."

Bill Dan nodded, but Roxie spoke out loud. "Yes, ma'am, they say the Old Dutchman slips back and catches everybody that tries to follow him into that mountain."

"What does he do when he catches them?" Letitia demanded, eyes wide.

"Shoots them."

Bill Dan digested the conversation, then discussed it with the others. It was hearsay; or was it? Undeniably, several men had mysteriously disappeared after saying they would trail the old man into his maze of canyons.

The maze began about forty miles eastward in that same broad, flat-topped formation with the weaver's needle in the middle of it, which the travelers had seen when they first neared town. They were still discussing it the next night with Lord Darrell Duppa, who had drifted into a close friendship.

"It is called Superstition Mountain," he explained, "because there are many superstitious beliefs about it. For one, the Indians say that the Thunder Gods live up there, and that they will destroy any mortal who goes into the mountain. I have heard these gods myself, as they pounded their gargantuan tom-toms. The roar echos from cliff to cliff and on down to here. It is very frightening and is always followed by slashing rains that swell our rivers. It flows right by the mountain, you know."

"Doggone!" murmured Roxie Webb with a very serious face. Bill Dan merely grinned at him.

All of them seemed glad and considered themselves fortunate that Lord Duppa had "adopted" them, Bill Dan reflected. He knew that the man was educated, refined, and that he had a fund of knowledge which was a continuing help to them. Mrs. Barry and Letitia were also educated to a degree. Bill Dan had enjoyed nine years of schooling, which was a lot, he himself knew. Roxie, who had been a servant back in Texas, could read and write and cipher. As for Leonti Soto — he was indeed a strange one, wise one moment and clownish the next.

Lord Duppa continued his story. "The white folk have their superstitions about the mountain, too — mystery tales, ghosts, Indian tortures, and the like. It is said that many a white man has disappeared on the mountain. That means not only the ones Old Snowbeard is supposed to have shot, but others before his time. Maybe the

Apaches who live up in the Four Peaks region beyond Superstition got them. Or maybe rattlesnakes, or thirst. Who knows?"

"Do you believe it all?" Bill Dan probed.

Lord Duppa shrugged and smiled. "I neither believe nor disbelieve. I really don't know. But the evidence keeps piling up, especially lately."

This conversation with Lord Duppa had taken place in late November. But Bill Dan, never one to say much, had also been listening to others, and Lord Duppa's talk renewed a stirring in him.

The talk was resumed out in the sunshine on the next Sunday afternoon. After a few minutes, Bill Dan rose and turned to take a long look at old Superstition. At this hour and from a distance the mountain was mostly purple, with lighter splashes of blue. The setting sun would turn it red and gold again, he knew. It seemed to be one solid pile of rock and was bare of trees, such as those which covered most eastern mountains, if he could judge by the pictures he had seen.

Presently Letitia turned and spoke to him, softly. "Bill Dan?"

"H-m-m-m-m?"

"You — well you are the head of our family. You know what I mean. I just want to say I don't *have* to stay in Phoenix."

He looked intently at the girl, frowning slightly as he did so.

"I merely said that I liked it here; I had friends. If you and the others, well, there's bound to be gold in

Superstition Mountain, and if you want to go up there, Bill Dan, then *I* want to go. I want to go where you go."

She practically revealed her heart, he felt. She had merely murmured the end of what she had to say, as she sat on a plank bench and looked up at the tall young Texan. No one laughed or smiled or even spoke; apparently the others sensed that this was a personal matter. As with one accord, they turned to gaze at the mountain, which was beginning to be tipped with gold. There was silence for a minute or more.

Finally Bill Dan stirred and said in a low tone, "People have started to call it the Lost Dutchman Mine. The old man was back in town again last week raising cain. Likely, he's sobered up by now. If you all don't mind, I guess I'll just walk down to his shack by the river and see what he has to say."

3

The Secret Map

Bill Dan hadn't gone fifty yards when he heard a jogtrot behind him, and he turned to see Roxie catching up with him. No rain had fallen for a month, so each time Rox dropped a shoe on the soft road soil, little puffballs of dust squirted out.

"You're kicking up a mighty cloud," Bill Dan said. "Apaches after you?"

Roxie grinned, his eyes lighting up his face as they always did. "Man, if Apaches were after me, I wouldn't be making no easy *plop-plop-plop* noise. I'd be going *whs-s-st zip,* like a streak of lightning."

Both young men laughed at the picture. "Me, too," agreed Bill Dan. "Coming to see the Old Dutchman with me?"

"No. Thought I'd cut over to George Austin's place to see if his sick cow got well. She had teat fever after bornin' her calf."

"Um-m-m-m." Bill Dan kept a serious face. "You wouldn't by chance be interested in anything else at the Austins? Like, say, George's daughter?"

Roxie's laugh was loud enough to be heard back in Texas. "That Ellen! Man, man! Whoo-o-o!" He angled left, calling over his shoulder, "See you back at supper. Maybe."

His departure left Bill Dan thinking about girls. He had met some pretty girls in Phoenix. Moreover, some of them were acutely aware of his presence. At the schoolhouse dance last Saturday night it had been plumb embarrassing the way girls had made up to him. Letitia's mother had giggled when she saw them. She said it was because he was not only the newest boy in town, but was also the handsomest.

"Oh, I don't know about that!" Letitia had countered as she danced away with Leonti Soto.

Leonti was as graceful as a year-old buck deer floating over a fence. Bill Dan couldn't dance for sour apples. Well, yes, he did know the steps for "The Texas Star," and "The Virginia Reel," but every time he had to touch a girl or put his arms around her waist, he felt shy. Of course, he didn't feel that way when the girl was Letitia. She was different.

Recently she had begun to dominate the women in Phoenix because she was educated and refined. He didn't have either of those attributes. She also had a knack for saying nice things to people and for making herself look nicer than any other girl he had even seen. Since arriving in Phoenix, she had done a mountain of sewing, and the way she looked on Sunday up there in the choir at the Brush Church was more than enough to keep his mind off the Reverend Bill Meyer's sermon.

As Bill Dan plodded in long, easy strides toward the Old Dutchman's, he tried to reassess his own personality — not that he was normally one to care or to be self-centered. It was just that Letitia had made him want to spruce up. So he had bought himself a brand-new Sunday suit that cost nearly twenty dollars. It was kept pressed, too, because Miss Nannie saw to that. And he had two pressed shirts and even new boots, kept shiny black with a mixture of tallow and soot from the chimney. He'd had a haircut, done by Letitia herself. While she was doing it, she insisted that he shave every Saturday, but she had let him, in fact, ordered him, to have a mustache. Her approach had been sisterly in such matters in the home, but he was hard put to keep the relationship on that plane.

"I'm whole Irish," she had said, "and you're half Irish and half Scotch, you say. Your red hair and black eyes set you off real masculine, Bill Dan. You look like the Governor of the Territory."

The terrible part of that remark was that six or seven of his friends had heard her say it. Those were the town boys who had been hanging around that Saturday afternoon. He had made up his mind that he would get even with her, or so he reminded himself now, grinning. The boys were starting to call him "Governor Allerdice!"

His meditation was broken abruptly. When he was about a hundred yards from the Old Dutchman's shack, he saw a Negro woman come out the front door, and she appeared to be agitated. People had said that Old Man Walz had a woman to "do" for him, to cook and clean occasionally.

She saw Bill Dan in the same instant and she came hurrying toward him. "Mr. Allerdice, are you coming to the Old Dutchman's house?" Apparently Bill Dan was known to her, which wasn't too surprising in a small town.

"Thought to, yes. Why? Is something wrong, or can I . . . ?"

"Yes, sir. He's a mighty sick man. I been bathing him, and he's got a high fever. Now he got a death look in his eyes, and I'm worried."

"Then a doctor. . . ."

"We only got a horse doctor in Phoenix, but maybe he'd know what to do."

Bill Dan frowned and showed his concern. "Yes, you go hunt for him, and I'll see if there's any way I can help Mr. Walz, meantime."

She hurried on, and he turned to enter the shabby, unpainted house. The place smelled of sweat, of illness and of age, of dust and ashes, and of stale cooking.

"Mr. Walz?" Bill Dan called.

There was no answer.

"Mr. Walz, I'm Bill Dan Allerdice. I dropped by to see if I could do anything to help you. Heard you been sick. How're you feeling, sir?"

He heard a half-moan as he tiptoed into the one small bedroom. The old man lay on a bed of rumpled quilts. His snowy hair and beard looked like a halo around his mas-

sive head. He was breathing slowly and noisily and his eyes were closed. Bill Dan knew instantly that the Old Dutchman was indeed a sick man.

He went closer, pulled up a creaky, unpainted chair of willow strips and rawhide and sat down. "Sir, I'd like to help if I can. Maybe you'd like a drink of fresh water? And a cool, wet cloth on your forehead?"

The old eyes opened a bit, but the man said nothing, so Bill Dan brought the water and a cloth. The Dutchman raised himself up enough to swallow a cupful of water, then lay back, waving the wet cloth away.

"Won't do no good to doctor me," he murmured. "I'm on my way."

"Sir?"

"You that boy with the Texas family? Shot up the Injuns that had 'em trapped? I heard tell."

"I'm with Mrs. Barry and some friends, yes, sir. We did have some trouble during nigh four months on the trail. But you, now, are you in any pain, sir? I could rub you, or maybe. . . ."

"No. No." He waved Bill Dan's hands away. "Nothing, son. I'm dying. Time to die, come to that. I'm old. Well past sixty."

"I've known men in their eighties, sir, so you just hold on tight and. . . ."

The old man ignored that remark. "You come to see me. You have come to see me when I am dying. You want to help me."

"I do for a fact. If you'll just let me try."

"No. I know when I'm at the end of my trail." The

old voice had become raspy and broken. "I'm beholden to you," he finally managed. "You, you're the only person that has ever . . . ever come to see me. Tell you what, son. . . ." His voice was close to a whisper now.

"Yes, sir?"

"Reach . . . under my bed. A box . . . wooden box . . . pull it out and. . . ." He had to pause and strain for breath.

Bill Dan, somewhat shaken with his own helplessness, reached under the bed as directed. "Here is your box," he said gently. "Is there something you want me to get out for you?"

"Open it."

Bill Dan lifted the heavy hinged lid. Three or four parcels wrapped in soft leather were in the box. There was also a fine pair of silver-mounted spurs which he knew were of Spanish or Mexican make. He wondered fleetingly where the old man had got them. One carton held smaller boxes of cartridges for a rifle, and another for a six-gun. There was also a rolled-up length of paper, faded and badly wrinkled. "What can I get for you, sir?"

He had to wait for the old man to force enough strength to speak again. "The paper . . . rolled."

Bill Dan took the paper out and unrolled it. It was a crude map.

"Look . . . careful," Mr. Walz rasped. "That's . . . Superstition."

"Yes, sir?"

"The mountain . . . east of here . . . I drawed that . . . needle in the middle. A peak."

"Yes, sir, I know. I saw it when I was coming to

46

Phoenix. It's like a weaver's needle or a Mexican hat."

"Yes," the old man spoke after a pause. "My gold mine is about half a mile from that. The key is a stripped paloverde tree." The old man spoke haltingly, and with great effort. "One big limb's left on, but it . . . it points *away* from Weaver's Needle."

The dying man exhaled hard from the effort, then lay still. Bill Dan thought the end had already come, but he doused the rag in cold water and mopped the old man's face. He wished the woman would return with the veterinary.

The old man coughed for a moment, then shaking and trembling, raised himself up in bed. The odor from his body was offensive, but Bill Dan tried to ignore it.

"Away from Weaver's Needle," repeated the old fellow. "Pointing away. You go . . . about halfway between it and the Needle, then about two hundred . . . yards to the east. Hidden there . . . is the richest gold mine I ever heard of."

In spite of his sympathy for the old man, Bill Dan Allerdice felt his blood racing. He knew that he had caught at least one of the old man's ailments — gold fever. He forced himself to remain silent and wait.

"People keep . . . trying to steal it from me . . . like I stole it first, myself." A pause, then the old man continued. "I was runnin' from Apaches. Shook 'em off . . . Then come onto . . . three Mexicans working a mine. The Hat Mine, they called it. Said they'd been there years before with a big party from Mexico . . . when they were boys. Peralta party. Miguel Peralta."

48

"Peralta, sir?"

Old Mr. Walz ignored the question and went on. "The Peraltas took out plenty of gold. Big horse train of 'em. Pack outfit. Loaded with richest ore." He paused to breathe noisily. "Got careless. Indians massacred 'em. Apaches. Only three boys escaped the killin'."

"Yes, sir!"

"They growed up and came back. I found 'em. Shot all three to get the mine for myself." He moaned. "Now I got to face God."

Bill Dan's impulse was to run back to town for the Reverend Bill Meyer, but the old man had grasped his hand, seeking a crumb of comfort in his last moments.

"I dragged their bodies to a crevasse and dropped them in . . . piled rocks down on top of them." He paused, but the Texan made no comment.

"I tried to share the mine with my nephew, he got to stealin' all our take-out . . . the nuggets . . . went to hellin' around." He paused to cough and spit and strain for breath. "One night in camp . . . I shot him. Put a chain around his neck and dragged him under a cliff by the river fording . . . buried him."

"Good Lord!" Bill Dan murmured in awe. His face was drawn, his eyes wide.

"Figured I better stay out of the mountain for a spell . . . let the talk and such die down. Last time there. . . ."

Bill Dan thought the old man was gone. Again he rallied.

"Covered up . . . the mine opening. Hid it good."

"Yes, sir?"

49

"Put heavy ironwood limbs across the top . . . piled rocks on top of that, and dirt. Then planted a cactus on the spot, but it mightn't live." The effort to speak was so weakening that his voice trailed off into a murmur.

Bill Dan's mind was racing. He couldn't feel any great sympathy for the old man, and he knew he'd have to report the confessed murders to the sheriff if the old man lived. It was an unpleasant duty. On the other hand, a man about to face his God and trying to clear his soul in the terror of dying. . . .

"In the box, son . . . open that . . . little leather bag."

With shaking hands the old man took the bag from Bill Dan, upended it, and poured out seven ragged-looking pieces of what appeared to be pure virgin gold into Bill Dan's cupped hands. One piece was the size of a silver dollar. Another was shaped like an egg, but flattened and jagged on the edges. Others were lacy and misshapen, but they were all beautiful. Bill Dan stared in awe at them.

"They're yours, son. To keep. Take the whole box . . . and all that's in it — spurs, from them Mexicans, pistol, map."

"But, sir!"

"That map — you can see where I drawed a horse's head. Look for it first when you go up there. Horse's head . . . rock . . . a cliff. That paloverde, with the pointing arm, it's barely half a mile from the horse's head."

"I'll take good care of all this till you get well and strong again, sir. I'll keep it safe and. . . ."

"You are the . . . only person ever to come and befriend me."

50

Appalled at his own helplessness, Bill Dan watched the old man die.

Slowly he returned the items to the wooden box. He covered the old man's head with a soiled quilt, then went to the door of the shack. There was no sign of the woman or of the veterinarian.

He knew that the Old Dutchman had no kin, no friends, so he closed the door and started away. "I'll just tell Roxie and Leonti," he said to himself, "and we'll dig a grave at the cemetery and bury him quiet-like in the morning. But I'll come back here and sit up with him for the night. Least I can do."

He had walked more than fifty yards when he paused. In the late twilight he stood for a moment, thinking. Slowly, he walked back to the bed of Jacob Walz, better known as Old Snowbeard the Dutchman, picked up the box and carried it to the home where he and his friends lived.

4

Departure at Midnight

Bill Dan was certain that the excitement he felt would show in his face and manner when he returned home. It did.

Letitia, who was sitting on the steps, spoke out as he neared her. "What happened?" she asked.

Leonti Soto was approaching the house from the corral. "*Oyez, amigo.* You been somewhere? *Que es?*"

Mrs. Barry looked questioningly at Bill Dan, too, and at the box he carried. The curiosity of the group was inescapable.

Bill Dan smiled slightly, went inside to put the box down, and came out to the steps. "All right," he said. "You all know that I went to see Old Man Walz, the Dutchman. I have to report now that he is dead."

"Dead!" Mrs. Barry exclaimed. "I declare!" she added as she shook her head in disbelief.

"Yes, ma'am. Found him bad off, sick." Bill Dan told of his visit and of his attempt to comfort the old man in his last moments. He did not, however, mention the story of the gold or of the gift.

He turned to Leonti. "I'd appreciate it if you would help me dig a grave tomorrow. He hasn't any kin. Rox is handy with carpenter tools; maybe he'd knock up some kind of coffin for him. I'll go over there and sit with the corpse tonight. We'll bury him as soon as we can in the morning."

Bill Dan and Miss Nannie quietly dressed the old man in Bill Dan's new suit, and before next noon Jacob Walz had been laid to rest in the little cemetery. Six other townsmen came to the graveside and heard Miss Nannie read briefly from her Bible, since the Reverend Bill Meyer was out of town.

Bill Dan reflected on how quickly a person could disappear from life with no one to mourn him. He went home, slept for three hours, then ate. Conversation was stilted and formal, he realized.

After Letitia had cleared away the dishes and returned to sit with him, she startled him by saying, "You want to tell me about it now?"

He stared at her in wonder. Finally he shook his head gently and smiled. "I'll never understand women," he said. "They read a person's mind. Very well, I do have something to say, but I'd better wait until everybody is here."

At the table after a late supper he told them. By that

time the sky had turned purple — broken only by a few spears of gold. A dove in a nearby paloverde tree was saying in muted tones, *"Low-oo, low-oo, oou so low-oo,"* and another species answered with a weird, raspy rattle. The eeriness seemed to set the proper mood for what Bill Dan was going to do. He brought his box to the table and slowly showed its contents with unconscious drama, speaking softly as he did so. Finally, he spread the map on the table, holding the corners down with heavy teacups.

Although he kept his voice calm and tried simply to repeat what had been said in the Walz cabin, a subtle quality of excitement in his manner created a contagion among his listeners.

"Bill-l-l *Dan!*" Letitia exclaimed. When she looked up at him, her violet eyes were wide.

"Mm-m-m-m, *La Mina Sombrera, seguro sí!*" Leonti Soto gazed afar as he whispered. "*Mucho oro!* Me, I go now start packing those wagons, all right? I have him hitch up before the sunshine arises. We leave in the dark, nobody knows, nobody follows, no trouble, soon we get rich, *si!*"

Roxie Webb spoke aloud. "You have said the truth, Leonti, my friend. You folks start packin'. We go grease the wagon, fill the water barrels, the canteens, put in some stock feed, the diggin' tools, the. . . ."

Bill Dan nodded. "We must move quietly, we don't want anybody around town to guess what we're up to."

"Now all of you just hold your horses," Mrs. Barry said.

"Ma'am?" All of them turned to look at her.

"You are the captain, Bill Dan. We made you our leader. But we can't afford to go off half-cocked. Stop and think, son. We have to take time to plan carefully and make sure that we go prepared. We can't afford to have gold fever ourselves."

A moment of silence followed before Bill Dan, feeling ashamed, said, "Ma'am, you are right. We have to keep our heads, just as we would if — well, if Indians were attacking. *¿Comprende, amigos?*" He had picked up bits of Spanish in recent weeks and used them unconsciously.

The friends understood. Instantly, their mood changed, the excitment subsided, and common sense took over again.

"Yes, sir," murmured Roxie Webb.

"Yes," Letitia added. "We have to make sensible plans."

"Seguro si." Leonti's tone had become sober. "What we do first? We don't talk from nobody, eh? We keep secrets. We take plenty time, we get ready. Is no hurry."

"That's exactly it," Bill Dan stated emphatically. "Now I was just thinking. It seems to me that we folks don't know all we need to know; we haven't actually had time to learn everything about this Arizona country. I guess it would take us a year, maybe even longer. We are ignorant in many ways. So. . . ." He paused, obviously considering.

"Yes, Bill Dan?" Letitia encouraged him.

They had drawn their heads closer to the two candles which flickered over the map. Again he felt that all eyes were on him.

"If you all agree — but not if you don't — maybe we might get our new friend interested in going with us. He has a good brain. He is educated; besides, he has lived here a long while; he likes us and we like him, and he seems to be footloose around here. He might like to go up to Superstition himself."

"Darrell!" Letitia murmured, her eyes brightening.

Bill Dan's lips set in a firm line. "Yes," he said, "Lord Duppa. What do you say?"

"I say, yes," Mrs. Barry was the first to reply. "He would also be one more gun for defense, if need be."

"That's so, I hadn't thought of that," Bill Dan nodded again. His face began to show a boyish eagerness. "Six rifles are better than five, if Apaches should come, though I don't expect they. . . ."

"Absotively!" murmured Roxie Webb. "Yes, sir. Me, I figure Mr. Lord Duppa a fine Confederate gentleman from England."

They smiled at Roxie's comment, then Letitia spoke. "Let's ask him, Bill Dan. Oh, I hope he will!"

Bill Dan wasn't too pleased about her enthusiasm, but he managed not to show any displeasure. He merely looked questioningly at Leonti, who was already nodding agreement. "*Si*. Six rifles. He no fool. And *mucho* for tell us, eh? *Muy bien*."

"That's right," said Bill Dan calmly. "We can learn a lot from him. And we all get along well. He calls us quality people, although I can't say just what he means by that."

"I can," said Letitia.

58

"All right then, it's settled. I'll ask him to come over here. I'll have to tell him everything, but I am sure there's no risk. He has something we need, and I think we have something that he needs, too. He has said as much."

Mrs. Barry nodded thoughtfully. "Friendship with people that trust and like one another makes for a sort of family. It's not to be belittled. Now we'd all better sleep on this idea and simmer down so that we can go about the business of getting ready without arousing suspicion."

"You are exactly right, ma'am." Bill Dan did not sleep well. He lay awake for hours, thinking. If those nuggets were a fair sample, there was no telling how rich the source strata might be. There could be enough to give each of them a lifetime fortune. Such a thing had happened in California. He twisted in his bunk, knotting a sheet under him uncomfortably. He was vaguely conscious of similar restlessness in Leonti and Roxie, who slept nearby.

It was Letitia who prodded him awake with a homemade broom.

"It's near nine, for goodness sake," she said. "You three are slugabeds. Breakfast is getting cold. Hoecakes and sorghum syrup."

As always, Bill Dan ate ravenously. By ten o'clock he was walking up the town's main street looking for Darrell Duppa. Since he wasn't out, Bill Dan went to his cabin and found him sitting under the roof of his thatched porch at a desk made of logs flattened and tied together with leather thongs. He was writing, but he put his pen back in its bottle of ink and smiled. "Morning, Mr. Aller-dice," he said. "You look fit." "Mr. Allerdice" was said in jolly comradeship; he and Bill Dan had some time ago progressed to first names. He leaned back in his willow-limb chair and stretched. "Come on, sit. How is it you are not at work? It's past ten o'clock."

Bill Dan grinned. "Could ask you the same thing, Lordy." As a token of friendship, they had so named the Englishman.

"I am busy composing poetry."

"Poetry!"

"Don't look so startled. Somebody has to write the world's poetry or there wouldn't be any. True, there are people who live it, rather than write it, but I am the lazy type. I woo the muse vicariously, I pursue culture on a synthetic plane — or something."

"Exactly what in the world are you talking about?" Bill Dan demanded. "You're just an Englishman, you're not the King of England. You got any coffee left?"

Lord Duppa had, and while the two sipped, Bill Dan announced what he was planning to do. "Lordy," he said, "we are all going up into Superstition, and we want you to go with us. We have a map to the Old Dutchman's mine."

Darrell Duppa put down his coffee cup and listened while Bill Dan told him the story in detail. "You know the Arizona Territory better than any of us. Besides, all five of us respect you and need you. Even your poetry," he concluded softly, glancing at the paper. "We don't have any of that, so you can read to us or recite some of it. You

60

can tell us things we haven't had a chance to learn. I would take on your expenses myself if you would come. I mean I'd supply your grub and ammunition and horses."

"No, sir," said Darrell. "I will supply my own. When do we start? I can be ready in an hour."

Bill Dan hurried back to the house to report the news. The others were delighted.

"How wonderful!" Letitia gushed, clasping her hands against her breast. "He's coming!"

Letitia's joy made Bill Dan glare. It struck him suddenly that he had been a fool. Whatever was he thinking to invite that foreigner along! Why, Darrell Duppa wasn't much older than he was. No more than twenty-two or three, and besides, he was too all-fired good looking! And a smooth talker, too. Thunderation, Allerdice, you've let yourself fall off the cliff!

Bill Dan tried to force his thoughts back to a more rewarding level, but abruptly the mental image of Leonti Soto appeared. Leonti and Duppa — both men would be bound to be attracted to Letitia Barry. Handsome Leonti with his black mustache and his ever-present smile. As for himself, his reddish hair had to be an inch long before anybody could see it, and besides, it didn't show much on his face, anyway. Even if he were to grow a beard, it would only look like scraggly fuzz on a puppy.

He decided to have the matter out with Letitia herself, so he followed her to their water well. He watched her pull up a bucket of water and drink from the bucket.

"Have some," she invited after she had finished drinking.

He drank the cool water, then plunged into what he had to say. "Have to ask you, Tisha. Do you, uh, feel anything about Lord Duppa? Or about Leonti Soto?"

Letitia looked startled, but without hesitating said, "Why, of course I do. They are fine men. They will be very valuable to us on our search."

"I mean, about yourself? You know what I mean. Two fellows like that, well. . . ."

"No trouble at all, Bill Dan. It's as easy to cook for six as it is for four, or even five. Mother and I can organize the camp routine in no time, and it won't be a burden. I thought you felt that Leonti was already one of us."

"I do, sure! I didn't mean that. He's my friend. He and Lordy both. What I was trying to get at, well, I mean. . . ."

"Stop worrying." Were her eyes twinkling as she said that, he wondered? "Bill Dan," she went on, "I can also darn socks and mend clothes and mold candles. We better be sure to put in plenty of tallow, and lantern oil, too. And I can reload cartridges and even shoe horses. So one more man in our party isn't going to work a hardship, you just wait and see. Besides, I like Darrell Duppa. He's refined and very pleasant to have around."

Letitia's endorsement was exactly what he had been afraid of. He grumbled "All right," and stalked off. If he lived to be a hundred, he would never be able to understand women or make himself clear to them.

He began immediately to work on his plan and to organize the group for its departure. This much, at least, he could do with confidence and skill. When he told Darrell about it, he tactfully made it clear that he, Bill Dan, was still their leader, even though the party had grown now to six. The two young men shook hands firmly on it, a gesture that made Bill Dan slightly ashamed for his moment of jealousy. He was proud to be liked and trusted by a man who could write and who could wear store-bought clothes every day. He was even happier when Darrell appeared in rougher clothes suitable for wear among desert rocks and thorns. The man was no sissy, for all his culture.

It was necessary that they provide necessities for at least a month's absence. It wasn't easy to do without arousing the curiosity of the townsfolk. Without actually being untruthful, Bill Dan tried to create the impression that he and his friends might soon push on toward California, as originally planned. Casually, but with no outward show of excitement, the group made a long list of needs, then began to buy a few things at a time, meanwhile seeming to go about their routine affairs in the village of Phoenix.

Wagon wheels had to be tightened, spokes and felloes set firmly, each tire made to clinch everything in its metal grip by soaking the rim in boiling oil. To do this took time, and Roxie Webb supervised the work. The shoes on the horses' hoofs had to be inspected, tightened, or replaced. Harness had to be strengthened and oiled against possible dry-air cracking, and extra leather and canvas had to be stored against need. In some instances saddle girths had to be rewoven. A new bit had to be fitted on a horse which Darrell Duppa had bought, a young gelding with promise of being very fast and intelligent. It had cost a fortune — nearly forty dollars. But a good horse was a man's most valuable possession.

The women helped to lay in the food supply. Both Irish potatoes and sweet potatoes were available, and all the members of the party loved them; besides, they kept well. Dried peaches, figs, apples, and blue raisins were on the market. Bill Dan loved to put a handful of raisins in his pocket to munch on as he worked. The men decided to buy salt beef, as the weather had been too hot in Phoenix to butcher hogs for bacon, ham, and sausage.

"We can shoot a deer anytime for fresh meat," Darrell reminded them, "and make any extra meat into jerky. And there's plenty of javalina, quail, doves, rabbits. We couldn't starve if we tried."

"I'll strip the venison for jerky," Letitia volunteered.

Cutting fresh, red meat into finger-sized strings and hanging them in the sun was an old border-country trick. In two or three days the meat would become hard and almost black and well-cooked. This "jerked" meat could then be softened in a nourishing stew or, if need be, just chewed and swallowed. Bill Dan himself had often made jerky while traveling, having first learned how to do it from the Mexicans in Texas.

Corn meal, flour, salt for both man and beast, pepper, coffee, brown sugar, molasses, soda powder, sulphur matches, flint and steel for emergency fires, water casks, blankets, cartridges, a new awl, also string and nails for boot repairs, a honing rock for knives, laudanum for possible stomach ailments, salves for sores and sunburn, laxative pills — the list grew, and soon the wagon bed was

64

filled. Where they were going there would be no stores, no source of supplies except those which nature offered.

The last evening they were in Phoenix a mad impulse hit Bill Dan Allerdice when he was in the town's general store. He toyed with the idea for several minutes before he spoke.

"Mr. Morris," he said to the storekeeper, "please, sir, wrap me up a dozen of them — those sticks of striped peppermint candy, in a separate paper, if you don't mind, sir. And maybe you won't happen to mention it."

Mr. Morris was not stupid. He winked at Bill Dan as he replied, "Wouldn't think of talking, son. A fellow wants to spark a girl, it's his business."

Bill Dan blushed and then grinned. When he finally managed to give the candy to Letitia that evening, she kissed him impulsively. She never mentioned the incident again, nor did he. But the moment stayed with him for days.

During their preparations, the party continued to let the townsfolk assume they they were about to push on toward California. That would mean, of course, that they would be going westward. Superstition Mountain lay to the east of Phoenix.

However, one midnight, with the women in the wagon and the four men on horseback, they pulled out of town as quietly as they could. Bill Dan Allerdice was leading them and heading west.

5

The Exciting Story

Swaying gently on his horse, Sam, and making as little sound as possible, Bill Dan began to inhale, then exhale deeply when his group was barely ten minutes from town. He lifted his face and smiled. A million stars, more or less, he guessed, shone in the clean, blue-black darkness overhead. Not only were they beautiful to look at, but they also cast just enough light in the moonless night for him and Sam to see ahead. He looked back and waved his hand. Letitia returned his salute from her seat in the wagon.

Darrell Duppa brought up the rear, about one hundred yards behind the wagon. Roxie and Leonti rode closer to the wagon. Nothing but the muted plop-plop of hoofs and the gentle creak of the wheels could be heard. After an hour of journeying, Bill Dan estimated that they were five miles from Phoenix, and since they

were now beyond the irrigated farm areas and onto the natural desert, he lifted his hand high.

"We'll begin to swing here," he spoke softly when the party had gathered. "Darrell, you take the lead. Roxie and Leonti, you be outriders. I'm going to tag behind and do what I can to cover up our turning traces with a mesquite limb broom."

Thus they moved off the westbound road and began a wide U turn, traveling over hard and rocky soil as much as possible so as to leave a minimum trail. Late-season rains had been showering the valley recently; Bill Dan hoped one would develop again today and erase any signs of them.

Dawn found them moving at a fast walk. Most of the area was reasonably smooth in this valley, although some trouble was encountered going around washes, boulders, and thick cactus growths. At 8 a.m. by Lord Duppa's huge sliver "biscuit" watch, they stopped for a quick breakfast of coffee, hoecakes, and the last of some slightly rancid bacon they had brought from town.

By noon they were out of sight of Phoenix and moving northeast toward Apache country. The high points of the mountains, called Four Peaks, could be seen about seventy miles away. Superstition Mountain was slightly to the right, and because the Apache Trail skirted its north side, Lord Duppa warned them to go into the mountain from the south. "It's much safer," he said.

Bill Dan agreed and swung their point. He kept two of the men as outriders all the time. Each evening he back-trailed alone because he wanted to be sure that nobody had followed them. Also, he was carefully checking for Indian signs.

As they moved fearlessly, yet cautiously, they could see Superstition's once-distant skyline loom ever higher and closer, gradually losing its hazy, purplish blanket and taking on a sterner aspect. A few trees became visible on its upper reaches, but it was mostly a maroon-red rock that seemed to push straight up like a fortress from the flatlands. It intensified the feeling of loneliness.

"Is nobody out here, *amigos*. Is nothing, but nothing," Leonti described it.

They understood perfectly what he meant, and Bill Dan nodded. It was indeed a wild, uncharted, but beautiful land. Late on the third day, he was scouting a mile ahead when he spied objects on the ground. He pulled Sam up abruptly, dropped reins, and dismounted.

For the next half hour he searched the earth around the area. Nearby against several huge boulders, he found definite evidence of old campfires under rock overhangs. Smoke stain showed on the ceiling stone and charred bits of wood were embedded in the soil. The fires had been burned many years before, he knew, but, by whom? Indians? "Not likely," he murmured to his horse, as he gazed at the objects he had picked up.

Slowly, thoughtfully, he remounted Sam, swung him around and walked him back toward the wagon. When he reached there, he ordered the folks to set up camp; then he displayed his trophies. "A rusted spur," he counted, laying each one in Letitia Barry's lap. "A metal stirrup with engravings on it. No Indian ever had such

things! Four rings. A rusty old pistol. And this!"

The last item was a finger-sized nugget of gleaming gold.

"Oh, Bill-l-l Dan!" Letitia breathed his name excitedly as she eyed the piece.

The others had huddled close. "That does it!" Lord Duppa exclaimed. "If we needed proof, this is it. Study these items, Leonti. Unless I am badly mistaken, they are of Mexican origin. Even the gold. That nugget has been molded. It has been crudely smelted, its ore melted in a pot, skimmed, then poured into a depression in a boulder to harden. It's a common process; it verifies the Superstition legend."

"How is that, Darrell?" Mrs. Barry asked. Even she was excited. "You think that the Old Dutchman may have dropped things when . . . ?"

"No, no." Darrell shook his head. "The Mexicans. I may not have told you folks the whole story of Superstition. We take a lot for granted around Phoenix, history, rumors, and such, you understand. We forget that you folks are new in the Territory."

"The Mexicans?" Roxie Webb questioned when Darrell paused.

The men began to sit crosslegged in a semicircle in front of Letitia, like young children awaiting a story. They were as eager as children themselves as they eyed the nugget.

"It starts with old Don Miguel Peralta, a rather famous rancher in the state of Sonora," Darrel resumed. "I expect you have heard of him, Leonti?"

71

"*Si, señor.* He's a big name in Mexico."

"Well, Don Miguel had a beautiful daughter, Rosita. She was courted by a young ringtailed tooter named Carlos, but before he could get around to paying his proper respects to Don Miguel and asking for her hand, she was pregnant. That made the old Don mad enough to start shooting."

"Quite right!" snapped Mrs. Barry. "Foolish kids."

"Mother! Please. Go on, Darrell." Letitia was excited.

"Well, of course, Carlos had to hightail it out of Mexico, so he fled northward. Don Miguel sent two expert Indian trackers to bring him back, dead or alive, preferably dead. They chased Carlos for weeks, but they couldn't catch him. He went hundreds of miles, evidently reaching the area where we are now, if the story is to make sense. Then one day the determined Indians saw Carlos running back toward them.

" 'Do not shoot!' the boy yelled at them. 'I come back. I have gold.' " Lord Duppa began to dramatize the story. "And, sure enough, he did have gold. His pouch and pockets were full of the richest nuggets these Indians had ever seen. They knew enough to realize that Carlos had found a bonanza, and that it would not only soften Don Miguel Peralta's wrath, but would also arouse his greed.

"To shorten the story, and it's supposed to be true, they took Carlos back, and the gold enabled Don Miguel to forget his anger. He organized an expedition and had Carlos lead it back up here. Sure enough, they opened a gold mine, which they called *La Mina Sombrera,* and took out ore worth thousands of pesos.

"When they returned to the ranch in Sonora, their news created great excitement. In a few weeks Don Miguel organized a bigger expedition, nearly four hundred picked men, to work the mine. Carlos had showed them that it was located in a long red mountain near a central peak shaped like the crown of a Mexican hat."

"We saw it! We saw it!" Bill Dan exclaimed. "It reminded us of a needle used in weaving, and Old Man Walz had named it Weaver's Needle!"

Darrel nodded. "The same. It has to be. Well, those Mexicans took out tons of ore and cooked it down in a crude smelting process, using natural little depressions in the boulders for molds. Look around, now," he said, as he swung an arm. "Do you see all those pitted rocks eroded by wind and rain and blowing sand? After skimming off the dross, the Mexicans poured their richer stuff in there to cool and harden. That's what you found, Bill Dan, that's what you have in your hand now."

He paused, and they began to study the sample again. They turned it over and over, feeling its weight and polish.

"This one got lost," Bill Dan suggested.

Darrell shrugged his shoulders. "Worse than that. The story goes that those Mexicans had started to pack their horses with leather bags filled with gold, but they got careless about safety — probably because there were so many of them. They weren't even ready to head for home when a gang of Apaches struck from ambush.

"From that point we can piece the story together ourselves. We know what must have happened. Both the saddle horses and the pack horses stampeded, scattering the bags of ore in all direction, for miles.

"The Apaches killed all the Mexicans except three servant boys who had hid under bushes. The Indians, no doubt, caught the horses, which they treasured. But they had no use for the ore, so they simply dumped it. Your sample is not the first of the ore concentrates to be found, Bill Dan. I have seen four or five others. Likely, they're scattered around, probably buried by time, winds, and rains. Nevertheless, they prove the existence of a very rich mine."

Bill Dan nodded emphatically, and the others stared wide-eyed as if hypnotized by the story.

"That story jibes with the one Old Man Walz told me," Bill Dan said. "He said he had murdered three Mexicans who told him they had come back to work the mine on their own! He admitted it right out."

Lord Duppa resumed his tale. "You have to realize that Arizona hasn't had many people living in it except Indians. The few who have drifted here either have not heard the story of the lost mine or have not been disposed to risk their lives searching for it. That is, until Mr. Walz started showing off in town. I think we may have an inside track, as we have some direct information and the map."

Bill Dan stood up. "All right, then," he spoke rather solemnly, "we'll move on up and do what we set out to do. But let's not daydream or be careless. We'll have to act with common sense."

6

Bars of Gold

For guard duty the four men split the nighttime hours into four shifts of two and a half hours each. Bill Dan took the last shift. It was a known fact that when Apaches attacked, they did so in the early dawn.

No one called him, however, when his turn came, and he slept soundly in his bedroll beside a big boulder until shortly after six o'clock when Letitia gently kicked his foot. At the touch, he jumped up, rifle at ready. He could have fired instantly at an attacker, having reacted from instinct and training.

Letitia was not alarmed. "Slugabed, put that rifle down; it might go off. I am not an Apache brave."

"Could have shot you. Might have!" he said, horrified at the thought. His hair was tousled, his shirt was wrinkled, and he gave off an odor of honest sweat. He stood in his socks, having removed nothing but his shoes at bedtime. He realized that he did not present a very romantic appearance.

Letitia giggled.

"What time is it?" he demanded.

"Six. But we must help Darrell to remember to wind his watch. Its winding key is so small that I made him tie a string to it and keep it looped to the stem ring, so that he can . . . ."

"SIX!" Bill Dan reached for his boots and glared at Letitia. "Why wasn't I called for guard duty?"

She smiled at him. "Hush! Mother and the others felt that you have been driving yourself. Each of them took longer shifts to let you sleep. They agreed you needed a good rest."

"Good rest, my foot!" He was not only disgusted; he was angry.

"And don't make a fuss, do you hear? They were doing you a kindness. Now go get yourself a drink of water, and come to breakfast."

He acted sullenly, but he obeyed her. He went to the water barrel on the side of the wagon and drew himself a scant cup of water. He could have wished for a face bath, even an all-over wash, but water was precious.

For breakfast Mrs. Barry had heated the cane molasses, so everybody swirled butter around in it on their metal plates to make a fine, streaked brown-red and yellow "soption" into which they dunked their slices of hot cornbread. As they ate, Bill Dan started to think. When he was about ready to speak, he discovered that Darrell Duppa's mind had been in the same groove.

"Say," Darrel spoke first, "if you should find one good nugget at the site of that massacre, and if it is true that those early Mexicans had bags full of them, then there certainly ought to be more around."

The others stopped eating. "Correct," Bill Dan nodded. "Was thinking as much myself. And a pile of golden nuggets wouldn't evaporate or wash away. Some might be covered by dirt and trash, but if we all went over there and searched . . . ."

They agreed instantaneously. They cleaned up the last piece of cornbread, set the camp to rights, loaded their horses, and started to the massacre site. It wasn't far away.

At first glance nothing of importance showed. A wild pig snorted and disappeared in thick jojoba and greasewood. "Javalina!" cried Leonti Soto, and ran off in a wide half circle. The others heard his rifle shot and, in a few minutes, he came back smiling, the first catch of fresh meat hanging down his back.

"He's small, so we can eat him up before he spoils," Mrs. Barry remarked happily. "I declare, a bite of fresh pork will be welcome."

The thought of food put all of them in a better mood, although Bill Dan began to worry that the sound of the rifle might have carried too far.

Roxie Webb, who had been ranging out a hundred yards or so and avoiding the stately saguaro cactus growths and the vicious cholla and prickly pear, came upon a strip of metal with two rings in it. It was plainly the top of a leather pouch. Nearby the metal was a small mound of dirt and gravel. He kicked at it and caught a glint of gold.

Together he and Bill Dan began to unearth the party's first major find — an assortment of small, smelted, misshapen nuggets of gold. None of them was larger than a man's thumb, and it was evident that they had been poured into the pitted boulders, cooled and molded right there. But a more important factor, Bill Dan said, was that it further verified Lord Duppa's fascinating tale.

The excitement was great as the men gathered the bars of gold, yet they all spoke in subdued tones. A rifle that had been shot to kill a hog could have been heard a mile or more away. Had there, by chance, been an Indian within ear range? Bill Dan hoped not, but he kept himself alert even as he fingered the treasure that Roxie had found.

Lord Duppa, who admitted that he knew little about ore concentrates, guessed that the find was probably worth about five hundred dollars.

"Our first gold!" Letitia whispered. "No, Bill Dan's nugget was the first. But this is a lot!"

Five hundred dollars did sound like a lot, in promise, if not in actuality. If there was this much in one spot, there might be more. They spread out to search, but only after Bill Dan had said he would circle the area on guard.

He stayed on guard for two hours, but saw nothing amiss. Twice he was tempted to shoot at quails, but the party had enough fresh meat for a few days. He moved cautiously, staying low, studying every detail of the Superstition apron, which was strewn with garnet-like boulders. In spots there were piles of dropped shale and dirt, and small rocks broken off from the cliffs. He saw nothing to alarm him, but he was glad when Leonti came to relieve him.

Roxie Webb, who seemed to have eyes to match a bloodhound's nose, had located two more spots where ore bags had been dumped. At one place the bags apparently had been scattered deliberately. Bill Dan and the others imagined that a young savage had grabbed the bag from a packhorse he had captured, opened it and swung it, strewing its useless contents over several yards. That possibility was verified by the pieces they were able to pick up which had been partly buried in the gravelly soil.

"About how many years ago was that Mexican expedition?" Bill Dan asked.

Lord Duppa stopped to think. "Well, not too far back. The story goes that the Treaty of Guadalupe Hidalgo gave the southern part of the Mexican Territory to the United States, and Don Miguel Peralta was afraid that you Yankees might not let him come up here much more."

"*We* Yankees?" Bill Dan was needling, but he was smiling.

"He's an American at heart!" Letitia came to Darrell's defense.

"Southern American," declared Roxie Webb and laughed.

Darrell ignored their comments. "Right after the treaty signing," he continued, "Don Miguel sent the final, big expedition up here to work the mine. The treaty was made in 1848, twenty-six years ago."

"Well, by the eternal," mumbled Bill Dan, "we've

stepped into something here, haven't we?" He resumed his searching, but found nothing, so at two o'clock they stopped to eat cornpone and greasy javalina accompanied by "salad greens," which Mrs. Barry had gathered from a now-dry wash near them. "I tasted some yesterday," she explained, "and I vow they are good for human food."

Later in the afternoon, both Leonti and Roxie found more gold; this time only scattered bits. Letitia also discovered two of the old, rotted leather pouches, both of which were full of ore. "They were buried in a pileup of thorny cactus nubs," she reported excitedly. "Nothing could have bothered them all these years."

"A pack-rat nest," Lord Duppa decided, after he had inspected the place. "Common desert critters. They steal anything they can, or they pile up thorny stuff around a homesite to keep out badgers, snakes, and other enemies. Lady, you have found a bonanza!"

Letitia's find occupied the party's attention until supper time, when Leonti was called in to eat, and Roxie replaced him on guard duty. Around their campfire, which was carefully hidden low in a gully, they inspected their stockpile of ore concentrates. They hefted each piece and guessed its worth. Some bits seemed to be pure gold; others were speckled with gold.

"Must be worth at least a thousand dollars," Lord Duppa declared. "And I don't want any share of it. You folks need it more than I do." All of them vetoed this idea, however.

"We are lucky cusses, all right," Bill Dan agreed. "If we went back home right now, we'd still be lucky."

None of them thought of going back, though. A treasure lay in their wagon, and a promise of a greater discovery of gold rode high in their hearts.

That night Bill Dan lay and gazed up at the brilliant stars. Somehow his thoughts began to turn to Letitia Barry. He began to speculate about her. For several years he had carried in his mind a vision of the "perfect" girl. After he had turned fifteen, this girl had been tall as a statue, with long, blonde hair and rather large features. But lately, in fact ever since he had rescued the folks from the Indians, the vision had become Letitia herself. The idea did not distress him; it interested him. The stirrings that the imaginary blonde had once set off lately had been intensified by the real presence of a brunette. These stirrings were strong now, and kept him awake for a long while. Soon, however, the need for sleep overcame him. Six hours later, he was awakened by Roxie Webb. "Bill Dan, you're due for night watch now. It's quiet out there —four or five owls snatchin' around catchin' things to eat."

"Thanks, Rox." Silently Bill Dan put on his shoes and started out, rifle in hand, while Roxie crawled into his own blankets. Bill Dan hadn't been out ten minutes before he became aware of a figure materializing against a red boulder twenty feet away from him. He wasn't alarmed, because he recognized it. He waited until it approached him.

"You haven't enough on," he murmured. "It's chily out here. Why aren't you asleep, anyway?"

Letitia ignored his question. "Mrs. Gray told me the paloverde trees turn into huge balls of yellow flowers in the springtime. I would like one or two put in my front yard."

A silence held. He made no reply as he tried to fathom her remarks. He was not too surprised; he had long ago learned that women talk in strange patterns, often irrelevant to anything at hand. So he waited for her to continue.

She had been staring into the darkness, but now she added, "We could put a rock bench under one of them, a settee, on the east side for late afternoon shade."

"Have you been to bed?" he queried patiently.

"Oh, yes. But my mind . . . . Bill Dan, I have never even seen a thousand dollars at one time in all my life; neither has mother. I want a rug on my front-room floor, too. I could make a pretty one out of rags, you know! I wasn't sleepy. I mean, I didn't want to sleep. I'll go back to bed now and dream some more. Bill Dan?" she whispered.

"H-m-m-m?"

"You may kiss me goodnight if you want to."

7

Dead Man in the Sand

The next morning at breakfast Bill Dan realized that the feeling of urgency had subsided. When they had first started from Phoenix, they had felt a sense of elation and hurry, as if the mystery gold in Superstition Mountain might somehow evaporate overnight. They had pushed hard the first few days, crowding their horses unnecessarily. This particular morning, however, he felt differently. "Any gold up there has been there for centuries, I reckon," he said to his friends. "We don't need to stampede ourselves. The mountain won't float off."

Letitia added, "I never get tired of staring at it. Just look at it now! It — well, it's not the usual kind of mountain, with one high peak sticking up. It looks more like a castle with turrets and spires. It's scary, because those cutback wings in the wall are such a dark purple that you just know things lurk there."

Bill Dan's mouth twisted scornfully. "What things?" he asked.

"Hush, Bill Dan. Horrid things! But it's beautiful, just the same. Such colors! Purples and blues and reds and streaks of yellow — it's like a petrified sunset!"

"You speak like a poet." Darrell Duppa smiled warmly at her.

His tone made Bill Dan smile wryly, and he persisted in repeating his question, "What things?"

Letitia ignored him and continued to stare at the majesty of the mountain against the rising sun. All she said was, "You can see proof of many deep canyons up there, Bill Dan."

Darrell Duppa, spooning hot cornmeal sweetened with molasses into his mouth, said, "I have been told that the mountain runs about thirty miles east-and-west, and twenty north-and-south. I doubt whether many people besides the Indians have really seen much of it."

"You said the Apaches regard it as a sacred place?"

"So I've heard. They think Superstition is the home of the Thunder Gods."

Bill Dan, making note of that point, went on, "Guess we might as well stay here a day or two more and keep looking for those ore concentrates. Might find another pile or two. Rox, you go out and poke around and yell if you locate another mound."

He and Roxie worked together, and the results, though not entirely bad, were disappointing. For one thing, the area was heavy with vegetation. "Whoever named this country as desert was 'tetched' in the head," said Lord Duppa. "I have seen the Sahara. My father took

us to Egypt when I was a youngster. This is not desert at all. Much of the time you are barely able to walk through this growth."

Letitia interrupted him, "I don't know the names of most of the things that grow here."

Darrell began to identify some of the flora that he knew. The others gave him eager attention as he poked his rifle at the beautiful cholla cactus, so thick with thorns that it looked ghostly in the moonlight. Each thorn had a barb like a fishhook. Bill Dan said that a clump of chollas seen at a distance in daytime could be mistaken for a herd of sheep.

Darrell went on to tell about brittle bush, called "golden hill," whose spring blossoms almost conceal its foliage, and of a smaller bush with heavier dime-sized leaves named jojoba. "It has these little nuts." He gathered a few as he spoke. "People grind them and use them like coffee. They're fairly tasty," he added.

"I'll make us some," Mrs. Barry said.

It was just at that moment that Roxie kicked what appeared to be a small stone about the size of his hand, flat and crusted with dried mud. On examination, it proved to be another one of the ore concentrates. Further nature study was suspended for the moment, and everybody began to search, eyes glued to the ground. Again it was Roxie who let out a shout.

He had been searching about thirty yards away from the others, so they gathered near him. He looked up in wide-eyed seriousness and exclaimed, "Dead man!"

Impaled on the muzzle of a rifle was a human skull.

The man had obviously been dead for many years. Roxie held the skull so far away from himself that Bill Dan began to tease him.

"Look out. I don't doubt it'll bite you, Rox. Just look at the white teeth! Where did you find it?" he asked as he took the skull in his hands.

"In another pile of trash under a prickly pear. Stuff all over it, except one white spot showing. I poked at it and . . . whoo!" Rox was surely putting on an act, and they knew it, but they seemed to be enjoying it.

Bill Dan concluded that a Mexican had been struck down at that spot and his skull had been covered over and had not disintegrated. By searching farther, they found a few more bones, including a heavy leg bone. It was badly eroded, and probably the flesh had been nibbled away by coyotes.

Since there was so little left of the skeleton, not enough to bury, they put the skull into their wagon and continued to search. Their spirits seemed dampened by the reminder of danger. Bill Dan decided this reminder could serve as a warning that their survival, not to mention their success in finding gold, depended on vigilance and down-to-earth thinking. That night he doubled the guard, keeping two men out in short shifts so that they wouldn't get sleepy and become inattentive.

Bill Dan himself did not report next morning for seven o'clock breakfast. Letitia explained his absence. "Last night he told me to say that he wouldn't be here until about noon. He said he wanted to look into something, but he wouldn't say what."

"He went off alone by himself?" Immediately Roxie Webb stood up.

"I wouldn't go after him," she said. "You know Bill Dan. He figures he's self-sufficient. He is, too, for that matter. Besides, he'd be hard to trail. You know that. And he'll be back soon."

"Something might get him out there." Rox glared off into space.

"Nonsense!" Mrs. Barry scoffed. "Not Bill Dan. I never saw a young man who could take care of himself any better. A body'd think he was thirty instead of twenty."

"He's nineteen," retorted Letitia.

"Nineteen, then. But he acts thirty."

"Only in some ways, Mother. He's really as shy as a little boy."

"Don't worry," her mother insisted. "He'll get over shyness, too. I doubt that anything could block Bill Dan for long."

They all worried silently until shortly after twelve o'clock, when an autumn sun was high overhead. Roxie's ears caught the click of a horse's hoof against rock about fifty yards away. Everyone lifted his rifle to be ready, just in case, and all of them hid behind boulders. It was Bill Dan who rode up and who greeted them. "I'm starved. Is dinner ready?"

The mid-day meal had been simmering in a big black pot — a savory stew which Bill Dan swore he had smelled five miles away.

Letitia Barry faced him, feet apart, hands on hips. "What kept you? Where have you been gallivanting to?" she said.

He pretended to look somber as he answered her.

"There's a girl who lives over yonder a ways. Tall, yellow hair with a pink ribbon in it, curly. Name of Miss Marguerite Smith. Pretty smile. She and I. . . ."

"Hush! Where have you been?"

He sighed audibly, winked at Rox, whose face had broken into a grin, then replied seriously, "Truth is, I had to check on something that Old Man Walz had told me. I don't think I mentioned this to you folks, but he said that one night he had killed his own nephew who had been trying to steal the mine from him. They were in camp close to a certain big red boulder with yellow stripes which was beside the Salt River, a kind of landmark place. Well, I saw that rock when we were coming out here."

"His own nephew!" Letitia was horrified.

Bill Dan shrugged. "He was a thief. So the old man up and shot him. Said he put a chain around the fellow's neck, dragged him to a spot beside that boulder, and buried him in the sand. It happened just a few months ago."

"He must've done just what he said," Bill Dan continued. "I dug in that sand. The body was too ripe to — well, you can guess what I mean. Some coyotes had already eaten some of it. So I just picked up the chain, washed it in the river, and put it on my saddle."

He brought the chain to them now, six feet or so of

half-inch metal links. The women stared at it, brows furrowed.

"It's good to know that the river," said Darrell Duppa matter of factly, "is not too far away. I see you washed more than the chain in it."

"I dunked me and Sam," Bill Dan grinned. "My hair had been dirty so long. And my. . . . He paused, blushed crimson, then muttered, "Sorry, ma'am," to Miss Nannie Barry.

"I hope you bathed good." Letitia helped him to save face. "We could all stand a bath. I wish this desert had more streams."

"Likely we'll find plenty up in the mountain canyons," Darrell told them. "I have heard of them. It rains up there, if not much in Phoenix."

"I needed to be sure Old Man Walz hadn't lied," Bill Dan explained. "So far, everything he told us has proved out. It means we likely can depend on his talk about the mine, too; the map and all."

That possibility struck a heartening note. It was gratifying, too, to realize that there had been absolutely no sign of Indians. The six of them might as well be in a place uninhabited except for themselves. As Leonti expressed it, "Is lonesome, is nobody out here." He spoke for all of them, for the vast emptiness was overwhelming at times. But loneliness was the curse of pioneers everywhere, Bill Dan reflected.

Here was a calculated risk, and Bill Dan felt optimistic. He knew that his friends would spend the afternoon searching for more of the ore concentrates. Unless their findings were unusually good, he planned to lead them away from this area the following morning.

"This spot is right smack in the Apaches' world," he mentioned, somewhat unnecessarily, to Darrell Duppa. "But Superstition is a kind of fort. Be glad to get up in there, myself."

Darrell agreed with him. The only safe and sensible thing to do, they decided, was to swing far around and enter the mountain from its south side, ten or twelve miles away from the Apache Trail on the north. First they'd search out the rock shaped like the head of a horse, next to the paloverde tree trimmed down to one pointing arm.

"The mine'll be right there!" Bill Dan mused aloud.

8

Hundreds of Horse Heads

Because the mountain served as a colossal screen to hide the sunrise until nine, the six o'clock breakfast hour seemed like midnight. They had to wait another thirty minutes after eating for light enough to be able to see around the cactus and boulders before they could start out on the next leg of their journey.

"No hurry," Bill Dan tried to comfort the others. Actually, he was as impatient as they were.

Much of their progress around the western and the southern apron was slowed by an incredible growth of the saguaro or giant cactus.

"I doubt anybody ever saw a thicker forest," Mrs. Barry said, leaning back to stare at a stately cactus plant more than forty feet tall. It had sixteen branches which, like the main trunk, were made of perpendicular accordion pleats, each one bristly with green-white needles two inches long. The plant had no leaves, but the tips of the branches bore drying "plum" fruits which were edible, even tasty.

The ten-mile push around to the south side of the mountain was slowed by so many thick growths and gullies that the party made less than six miles before nightfall. The following morning's travel was somewhat easier. By noon, Bill Dan, who had been scouting ahead, found what he called a natural gateway into the south side of Superstition. He swung Sam around to gallop back to the others.

"Up yonder a mile," he shouted back, "is a mess of red-yellow boulders that must've dropped off the cliffs some years back. They're bigger than courthouses; some are like stores piled on top of each other. We can wind a trail up through them to the foot of a steep cliff that must be nine miles high. Come on!"

"Bill Dan, wait!" Letitia caught his enthusiasm. She had been on foot at the moment, but now she unhitched her mare from the rear of the wagon, swung to the saddle, and galloped ahead to join him. Mrs. Barry was driving the wagon, and Darrell was far out on scout duty. Roxie and Leonti brought up the rear, and were guiding the animals through thick cactus growth. The party had brought along fourteen horses in all: two to pull the wagon and a spare saddle for each person. The extra horses carried packs, and at times they were lashed together with long ropes.

"It's so beautiful here!" Letitia exclaimed, riding up alongside Sam. She reached over to pat Sam's rump, but her Molly nipped Sam's shoulder to force him behind her.

Ignoring the actions of the two horses, Bill Dan remarked, "Best thing is, we have shelter."

"Shelter? What kind?"

"Natural." He pointed to the magnificent red cliff face now shading to blue-purple. "Right at the base of that. Fall-off rocks, leaning over one another. Wind and storms have hollowed some of them out. Others have piled on top of each other, so there are actual rooms for us to live in. Rooms, like those in a house; or like caves, only nicer. There are places for the horses, too. And there's one for the wagon. Wouldn't have believed it — man-a-mighty!"

He was high with excitement this morning and was glad of it. He smiled at Letitia and again shouted, "Come on!" He could have been a boy, aged thirteen, playing tag.

Almost immediately, though, he quieted down, became a man again, and "studied out" their potential homesite. With Mrs. Barry he chose a "living room," in reality a cavelike depression facing south with overhang and walls on three sides. It was larger than their entire dwelling in Phoenix.

The women were delighted to find the place swept clean of leaves, thorns, and trash blown by wind. Time had packed the floor hard, and it rolled ever so slightly. Here was a fine place to put duffel from their wagon. Back against the curving rear, Bill Dan suggested that they pile dry grass and make a mattress. Soon he'd drive pegs into the rock-wall cracks on which to hang things.

Within twenty yards of the first cave they found accommodations almost as good for the men; sheltered overhangs, more rooms formed by the rocks where bed-rolls would be safe from rain, water drainage, and winds, and at the same time let in the winter sunshine. The wagon was backed by hand under one huge boulder which was propped slantwise over two others. The horses could be stabled and corralled among other boulders, simply by stretching two ropes across a natural entryway.

"But the best thing," Bill Dan exulted, smiling at his companions, "I have not told you about. I imagine Lordy has found it while scouting around out there. But come here." He led off, beckoning to them to follow.

They went around fifty feet of sloping, gravelly soil, then down a sharper slope about twenty feet among knee-high rocks covered with green cress and ferns.

"How's this for luck?" He pointed to a water hole. "Sweet water, not saltish at all!"

Much western water was brackish, they knew; sometimes it was unfit to drink. This pool appeared to be ten feet across and at least four feet deep, and out of it trickled a streamlet as big as a man's arm.

The women emitted shrieks of gladness and dropped to their knees. The men soon joined them. The long drink, the wet faces, the happy smiles showed their pleasure.

"I can live here forever," Letitia said clasping her hands together in a characteristic gesture of enthusiasm. "What a view!" She pointed southward. Although they had not realized that they had been climbing, they saw that their homesite at the foot of the cliff was at least three or four hundred feet above the sweep of the valley. Half of Arizona Territory was spread out before them.

"Forever," Letitia repeated, and Mrs. Barry nodded in understanding.

"That's a long time," Bill Dan smiled, "but I know what you mean. However, we've got work to do before 'forever' comes around."

It was a subtle command that was not wasted on them. Time was required to set up this camp as it was likely to be their most permanent one. From here they would search out the Lost Dutchman Mine.

First, the three men not on guard duty gathered dead limbs from the undersides of the mesquite, ironwood, and paloverde trees. They added dried grasses and leaves and piled them on top of a boulder within easy access.

"If you need to call us," Bill Dan explained to Letitia and her mother, "any time, whether it's Indians or an accident or what, just light this pile of brush. After it starts blazing, put this other pile of green foliage on it. That'll make a black smoke column that we can see for ten miles at least. We'll come a kiting!"

He led Roxie and Leonti and Darrell to a second rock about fifty yards away, on which they built a second pile of trash and limbs.

"One fire, one column of smoke," he explained to the women, "will be a signal for everybody to return home. It might mean just an accident, a broken leg or something. Or it could mean an Indian attack."

"And the second fire?" Letitia asked.

"Light both fires if the rest of the party should run! I mean — well, I guess the only place to which we could run would be Phoenix. For example, if you had to take off in a hurry and wanted to telegraph the message to the others, we'd all run like scared rabbits, maybe, and hope to meet safe again back in town."

The signal fires afforded a bit of comfort. Making the camp, settling in, arranging everything for convenience — all this took hours. They did not start to search for the Old Dutchman's mine until the following morning.

The men drew straws at breakfast to see which two would search first, and Bill Dan and Darrell won. Leonti rattled off something in Spanish, which caused Darrell to chide him for swearing; whereupon the Mexican apologized, picked up his rifle, and said he'd stand guard duty until noon. That left Roxie standing, his face a picture of despair.

"Stop glooming," Bill Dan ordered his friend. "You've got it easy, man. While me and Darrell have to face dangers from an unknown trail, with likely wild cougars, bears, maybe even Apaches, you can stretch out in the shade and snooze while . . . ."

Roxie hit him on the shoulder with his fist, and Bill Dan ran off laughing to saddle Sam.

"I'd be as mad as Roxie and Leonti if I hadn't won," he confessed to Darrell as they saddled their horses.

They had already picked a starting route. It led off first to the east, then circled sharply uphill and around a fortress-like projection about three hundred feet high. Once they got around it, they could see a half-dozen cuts and canyon avenues into the main bulk of the mountain. These obviously had been drainage areas that had been centuries in forming. They picked one that seemed to lead directly toward the mountain's center, so Bill Dan pointed Sam's nose that way.

The horses had easy pickings for a while, enabling the men to talk, although they instinctively spoke in low tones and stayed close together. Sounds carried far in the thin, pure air.

"It isn't likely that Old Man Walz was just teetotally running off at the mouth," Bill Dan repeated, for maybe the thirtieth time since Jacob Walz had died. "We have proved that he wasn't lying in other things, so why would he about things up here? I vow he really did cover up that mine and mark its location, just as he said."

Darrell nodded. "Hope so, anyway. And that means we had better locate his Weaver's Needle first, as a starting landmark. But look alive, Bill Dan. We, too, could get lost up here."

The Texan and his friend began to take careful note of directions against standout rocks and peaks. Also at Bill Dan's directions, they decided to put a huge stone on top of the nearest shoulder-high boulder whenever they came to a major split in a new trail. This marking could guide them back toward home; it could even save their lives.

Their horses were almost belly deep in grasses and shrubs. One upland area, which was as flat as a small corral, was covered with clusters of green things that looked like buggy whips fanned out from a central root. These, said Darrell, were the "wands of the winds," called ocotillo. The "wands" ranged up to fifteen feet long, and were covered with vicious-looking thorns.

Around eleven o'clock the two men decided to tether their mounts near a deep water hole they had found, then proceed on foot, as the going had become too rough for the horses. Each man took a half-gallon canteen, his pocket pouch of food, his belt knife and his pistols, his rifle, and his courage in hand, then started walking.

Surprisingly, after a quarter-hour climb the going was much better. The stark rocks seemed to have tumbled down the slope; the mid-level plateau and the ground beyond were smoother, and there was less foliage.

"Gosh, but it's pretty up here!" Bill Dan exclaimed. "Tisha and her mother sure will be excited."

An hour later they had reached a tight crevasse between two ancient cliffs through which the sky seemed like a shimmering thread above them. Moving cautiously, and breathing hard because the air had thinned more, they came to the end of the near tunnel, stepped out on yet another plateau.

"Sa-a-a-a-ay!" Bill Dan murmured in awe.

Both men paused, lowered their rifles, and stared.

Across a deep, upper-mountain canyon, not more than a quarter-mile away by direct line, and exactly on the level of their eyes, they saw that great central Superstition landmark which the Old Dutchman had named Weaver's Needle. It looked to them to be one solid chunk of granite. It almost touched the sky, its point pink-gray and glistening with dots of mica, and silhouetted against a bank of clouds edged in turquoise.

It took the two men ten minutes just to drink it in. It was Darrell who finally spoke. "So all right, then, my friend," he said, "we have our starting point. All we have to do is to locate the cliff outline that shows a horse's head, then a paloverde tree trimmed down to one pointing arm."

The sheer majesty of Superstition Mountain still hypnotized Bill Dan. "I'd like to climb it. I could, too! If I had time, I would take and . . . ."

"That's exactly what you haven't." His friend brought him back to earth. "You are not up here on a Sunday-school picnic; we are out to find ourselves a stake in life. Right?"

Bill Dan grinned at his friend. "Yeah, I know. So let's start looking." He squinted at the sun and then at his own shadow. "It must be past noon. We better eat, then start working again. Darrell, we could look at it while we eat, and that would do no harm, hey?"

The Englishman smiled and slowly shook his head as if to say that Bill Dan was irrepressible. But he sank down into the low autumn grass, took a drink from his canteen, got out the sandwiches which Letitia had made and bit off a mouthful of bread and cold pork.

They ate without making conversation. Bill Dan was still entranced by the sight of that peak. Afterward, though, he lay back on the grass, covered his face with his hat, and slept for ten minutes. Darrell understood and followed suit. A restorative snooze could quicken perceptions and sensitivities. The two men were anything but lonely in this vastness near the sky. They felt as if they were one with the universe, and they awoke later immensely refreshed.

In five more minutes, they had separated to go in opposite directions to scan every cliff edge and every rock face for a form that would suggest the head of a horse. They would meet one hour later at a designated spot.

Bill Dan moved silently as he had learned to do from long experience. Although he had no sense of danger, he carried his rifle at ready. He felt it unlikely that any Apache would be within range; there simply was no logical reason for Indians to be at this place. Not only was it holy ground to them, but it was too inaccessible. Any game killed here would be hard to pack down. Water was present, but that alone was no lure. The Indians were not interested in gold, so he felt that he could safely focus his eyes on the cliff formations.

For the first twenty minutes that he looked, not a single straight-up edge of rock, not a cliff face eroded into bas-relief even remotely suggested the outline of a horse. Then suddenly he saw one that looked like two horses. One was a roan which was kicking up its heels. The other was an old hammerhead gray-blue with head and neck showing. No, that formation was actually more like a deer, for even the antlers could be seen, and the nose was too short for that of a horse.

He walked on for another half mile, looking and studying every bit of scenery. Bill Dan began to find a horse's head in almost every direction. Funny, he admitted wryly, what imagination can do. He grinned, tight-lipped, at himself. Then he decided to sit down a moment, take another drink of water, and start out afresh. Likely then,

he would see the special horse head which old Jacob Walz had meant. He was sure that it would stand out, a sight that couldn't be mistaken, once it was identified.

At the end of the hour, though, he and Darrell had met again, and each had to admit that he had seen only mountain scenery in general. Darrell, too, had imagined he had seen a horse on every cliff. In addition to horses, each also reported identifying cows, Indian chiefs, elephants, even churches complete with steeples, carved "perfectly" on the sky-high faces of Superstition Mountain.

By three o'clock in the afternoon they had begun to concentrate on finding the paloverde tree with the pointing arm.

The paloverde rarely showed much of a central trunk, but its branches seemed always to twist up from its core and fanned upward for perhaps six to fifteen feet. Hundreds of little branches grew from the core, and hundreds of thousands of twigs grew from the branches. The result was a thick lacing of little straight lines as if they had been sketched with a green pencil on paper. There were no leaves on most of the trees. Darrell said that nature had long ago dried up the leaves of nearly all major desert plants, converting the leaves into twigs or thorns, so that precious moisture couldn't evaporate so easily in dry air. He explained that it was a way nature's plants had of adapting to desert conditions.

He and Darrell, fatigued by walking and by the altitude, sat on a rock to discuss the situation. They could look in any direction and count endless paloverde trees, not to mention thousands of other mountain growths. The palo-verde they were looking for might be hidden by boulders. Jacob Walz had said it was about half a mile from the Weaver's Needle, but that took in a lot of ground. Also he had said that the arm pointed away from the Needle, not toward it. And two hundred yards from the east of that tree was the richest gold mine any mortal ever heard of.

No wonder the two young men were racked with impatience and disappointment. That tree had to be found. This was the moment in which they should have been excitedly filling their saddlebags with the nuggets they had discovered after taking away the planted cactus, the dirt, and the ironwood logs from the Dutchman's mine shaft.

But by six o'clock Bill Dan and Lord Duppa, slumping dejectedly over the backs of their horses, plop-plopped slowly toward home camp. Letitia, who had been on the lookout for them all afternoon, ran out to greet them. "Hi!" she called.

Bill Dan raised a lanquid hand in answer. Sam was plodding faithfully along, but something in the manner of the two men must have telegraphed the news to her.

When they stopped, she spoke again. "You didn't find it."

To Bill Dan her eyes looked much bluer than the Superstition skies. Her cheeks were flushed, too, and she appeared beautiful and desirable. He hated to disappoint her, but he shook his head negatively.

"Maybe tomorrow," she said, forcing a smile.

9

Alert for Ambush

That night Bill Dan was exhausted. His weariness worried him at first, as he had always thought his energy was boundless. Many times he had ridden or walked or worked twice around the clock without feeling as tired as he felt now. "I must be coming down with something," he told himself silently, although he resolved not to show it. He couldn't remember ever having been sick before. Finally he mentioned his symptoms to Lord Duppa.

"Nothing the matter with you," the Englishman answered "except in spirit. We're both bone tired and disappointed. We aren't used to so much walking in thin air at mile-high altitude, that's all. Go to bed."

Bill Dan welcomed the command. The women had fed him well, and with Roxie helping, they had gathered dried grasses to make thick mattresses for the men, which they put back against the sloping wall under their bed-

room overhang. It took Bill Dan just thirty seconds to snatch off his heavy shoes, slide down between his blankets, inhale the fragrance of the hay and fall asleep.

He doubted he had even moved a muscle before Letitia called him to breakfast. He got up, feeling as fit as a fiddle, and said so, but he was angry because Leonti and Roxie hadn't called him to take his turn at night watch.

"You can make it up to us soon," they warned him. "There'll come a time."

They would take their turn in the rugged mountain today, so he would let them sleep it off tonight.

At breakfast Letitia showed that she was worried about him. "I declare, Bill Dan Allerdice, how can a body ever eat so much? You had a hearty supper, I know. And all you've done since then is sleep. Where do you put all that food?"

"Let him alone, dear," her mother chided. "Men need a lot of food."

Bill Dan tried to ignore their remarks. He blushed a little, and said, "*Miss* Barry, if you and your mother wouldn't cook so good, then we men could see our way not to eat so many rations. But as it is . . . ."

"You see, dear?" Mrs. Barry said. "He's Irish. That was pure blarney. And don't tell me you don't like it."

The others joined in the teasing, meanwhile chuckling, eating, and slurping their coffee softly to cool it. There was a happy fellowship in the sunrise chill. They sat cross-legged in a circle facing a bed of glowing coals. When they had finally finished eating, Bill Dan and Lord Duppa brought in flat pieces of sandstone, which weighed about twenty-five pounds, and laid them on the ground near the fire. Bill Dan beckoned for Roxie and Leonti to look over their shoulders while he guided Lord Duppa to scratch a map on one of the stones.

"This is us," he began, making an X. "Our camp is right here. Now, Lordy and I started off this way, northeast, then circled back almost northwest around that first big cliff." He was sketching, and he paused to point. "We rode uphill, maybe five miles, wouldn't you say, Lordy?"

Darrell nodded. "Four or five at least. Rough going."

"To about here." He made another X on the rock. "We staked the horses, then went on foot through several canyons and out onto a high-level shelf where we saw that Weaver's Needle. And I'm here to tell you it was a pure sight! You can follow our tracks easy, because we didn't bother to hide them; we trampled down lots of grass and we made rock-on-rock signs. And from there we scouted that part of the mountain looking for a cliff showing a horse's head." He went on in detail, reporting on their efforts, their frustrations. Leonti and Roxie asked many questions.

"Best we don't go where you went," Roxie suggested. "We'll look somewhere else. I bet we find both! That rock horse, that paloverde. Maybe we'll find the mine itself." He grinned, his white teeth flashing. Obviously, he was afflicted with gold fever, Bill Dan realized.

"All right; hope you do," he smiled encouragingly.

Leonti then spoke. "Me, I find heem, I let out yells you hear in Mexico!"

When the two had ridden away, Bill Dan and Lord

Duppa split the day for local guard duty. Bill Dan drew first shift. He picked up his rifle, but put it down to help Letitia gather wood for cooking and for campfire warmth at night.

"Get ironwood mostly," Mrs. Barry begged them. "I declare, it's God's gift. It's so heavy it won't float in water. And it makes a fire hotter than coal used to do in a blacksmith shop. Even the twigs are worth gathering."

"Ironwood is rightly named," Bill Dan added. "Hit it with an ax, and the blade just bounces off. But it's brittle; it'll break up even if it won't cut."

In a few minutes he vanished silently into the thick verdure growing near, but presently he began to hum as he studied the landscape. He had no fear; he expected no Indians or other trouble. He wished he could be back up the mountain, searching. He'd give anything to be the one to find that mine, or at least be there when somebody did find it.

When he was out a quarter of a mile from camp, he began a slow patrol in a semicircle. Most of their lookout would be from spots to the westward, on the premise that any Apaches would naturally approach from that direction after circling the front of the mountain. But he kept telling himself that he had no reason at all to expect them; they would not suspect the presence of anyone near Superstition Mountain. His party had moved with great caution, and the chances of their trail's being cut back yonder on the flats were remote.

His peaceful mood was enhanced when doves began to "talk" to him, or to each other. Back in East Texas he had known about doves, but hadn't often seen them; the bobwhite quail dominated bird life down there. Quail were here by the thousands; they were friendly, trusting, innocent-looking. Anyone could walk within ten feet of them before they'd fly off.

Nature's special exhibits intrigued him further when he stepped over a low-cut gully which had recently held water. There he stooped to pull up a bulb of wild garlic. He peeled back the outer skin and decided he'd eat it right then, but he wished he had a piece of meat to go with it. He stared at the pretty bulb, then popped it into his mouth. The taste was disappointing; it was too potent. He spewed it out, but he plucked half a dozen more bulbs and stuck them in his pocket to take to Miss Nannie for seasoning. He wished he hadn't tasted it; the heady fragrance seemed to go up his nostrils and even into his brain.

His brief moment of meditation was interrupted by a feminine voice calling him. "Bill Dan."

He was embarrassed and angry at himself. A man's interest in his stomach could have lured him to his death! One garlic bulb had so distracted him that Letitia Barry had slipped up, unseen and unheard. She might just as well have been an Apache with tomahawk lifted. She was coming slowly, carefully avoiding the thorns.

"Hi," she said, and smiled when she got close to him.

"You could have been shot," he rumbled.

"Isn't it a glorious morning!"

"Slipping up on a body that way! You know better than to be out here by yourself. Anything could happen. Why'd you come?"

113

"Darrell said so, too."

"Huh?"

"What in the world is that horrid odor?"

He felt a flush rise on his neck, but he ignored the question.

"You ought've stayed in camp, anyhow." But he spoke more gently this time.

She had begun to cast a spell on him. He could work with her or near her all day, and nothing would happen. Then the next minute she would turn on some kind of an inner something and he melted. He stared down at her, noticing how her black hair fell to her shoulders and bounced up again like a waterfall. Her eyes looked much bigger than usual, too.

She brought him out of his trance by continuing matter-of-factly. "Anyhow," she said, "I brought my rifle, and I have my pistol strapped on. I can shoot nearly as fast and as accurately as you can, Bill Dan. So really, we are two guards out here instead of one. Did you get rested from your hard trek yesterday?" She almost purred.

He smiled, his angry nood now forgotten. "Me? I feel so good this morning I could climb a cactus holding a wildcat under each arm."

She smiled back at him, and the thought flashed through his mind that what he had said was silly. But he did feel good. He felt not only good, but reckless. He felt his shoulders square back, and he managed to let another smile cross his sun-bronzed face. You're a lucky dog, Allerdice, he told himself. Soto's gone up the hill. Duppa's at home writing poetry or something, and you,

Bill Dan, are out here alone with this girl. "Uh . . . how're you feelin'?" he questioned, in a conspiratorial tone.

"Fine! Bill Dan, I am very happy out here on Superstition. The happiest I've ever been — with mother and you four boys. You have all become like brothers to me. It's enough to make any girl happy."

Her last comment broke the spell so much that he was almost angry again. But he quickly got hold of himself and smiled back. He tried to stay a few feet from her. That garlic still tasted awful and smelled worse, especially contrasted with her delicate fragrance. He felt a powerful urge to touch her, yet he didn't quite dare; he was afraid he might let himself get out of hand. Anyhow, garlic and romance didn't mix.

He stood glaring at her as he watched her look starry-eyed across their world of beauty. And in this heart-to-heart silence he caught a slight sound. He caught it more or less instinctively, because his senses had long been trained to be alert. First, there was a slight swish, then the faintest click.

His mind flashed the knowledge that it must be a person, probably an Apache, in spite of their fancied security. The motion and the sound had come from a brushy area not fifty feet from them. That faint click — it had to be the sound of a man cocking his rifle.

At the instant of the sound, he pulled Letitia low to the ground, his rifle at point, his heart pounding.

Bill Dan swore to himself. He deserved to be scalped because he had not been paying attention. His attention to Letitia had let themselves in for trouble.

In the silence that followed the motion in the shrub-bery, Bill Dan figured that a century had elapsed. Eventually he began to breathe again. "Sh-h-h-h-h, don't move!" he cautioned Letitia in a whisper.

His mouth was just above the top of her head. Their rifles were at ready between them. He knew he must wait until a definite target could be seen; it wouldn't do to waste the first shot. He strained for a glimpse of the enemy and wished he could comfort Letitia. He blamed himself for getting her into danger. True, she had come on her own when he was on guard duty, but he could have made her go back. He hadn't wanted to, of course, for he treasured their moments together.

Strain as he would, he could see no one. They waited and waited and waited. Hours seemed to pass. Then their silent wait was repaid and they heard the rustling of shrub-bery repeated. It was not really a noise, just the barest hint of motion. Apaches rarely had rifles, he had been told, but it was possible that they could have taken them from slain white travelers. Bill Dan figured that if he or Letitia moved, the imposter would fire without actually seeing his target. So their only hope was to fire first. Slow-ly, silently, he lifted his rifle to eye level. He dared not cock it yet — the click would be too revealing — but he would cock and fire as close together as possible. After another long wait, he finally saw the jojoba bush move again.

His rifle shot was loud. He felt Letitia jump to the left and, at the same instant, he rolled to the right. They

116

did this instinctively, knowing that the rifle burst would pinpoint them as a target.

Instead of an answering shot, there was a lashing noise and Bill Dan knew grimly that he wounded, maybe killed, a man.

The lashing in the bushes stopped, but he and Letitia caught the sound of something falling, and then of a deep, half-cough, half gasp. At that moment the bushes parted, and the victim plunged out and fell with a crash.

10

Ancient Village

"Bill Dan, look!" Letitia shrieked. "It's a deer."

Blood spewed from the chest of a young, six-pronged buck. Together Bill Dan and Letitia hurried to the animal. Bill Dan said nothing. He felt elated and also ashamed. He had been so wrapped up in a pair of violet eyes, a smile, and a bit of chitchat that he hadn't let his senses work to their full capacity. He wished he could kick himself. "You — you all right?" he finally managed to say lamely.

"Of course! Aren't you? How lucky we are to have fresh meat again."

"Plenty of deer around. Could've shot one any time. But I. . . ."

"Hadn't we better start to dress this one? Maybe just cut out the entrails so that I can get the liver, then we can both carry him home for skinning. He isn't terribly heavy."

Trust her to be sensible, when he was not. He lowered his rifle and got out his belt knife. To slit the carcass wasn't much of a job. It would have been easier if he could have lifted the buck's hind end on a rope, but he managed. He slit the center of the white-haired belly as Letitia watched. The membranes and the tissues were strong. Finally, with her help, he hefted the gutted animal onto his back and held the horns. Letitia carried the liver and both their rifles and they trekked their way back to camp.

"When I saw that bush move and heard that click, I thought it was a rifle cocking, . . ." Bill Dan said.

"Yes. But I guess the deer's hoof touched a rock. Maybe he knocked one rock against another. It's because our nerves are on edge. A good thing, I suppose."

When they were within fifty or sixty yards of the camp, he looked up, expecting to see Darrell Duppa or Mrs. Barry, but neither was in sight. "Where are they, do you reckon?" he said.

"They have to be around somewhere," Letitia said. She was leading and they trudged on, but instinctively she lifted and cocked one rifle.

They had to walk around the last big boulder before they could see anyone. Then Mrs. Barry called to them. "Land sakes! You scared me out of my wits!"

"Mother, Bill Dan shot us a fine deer."

"I thought we weren't to do any shooting near home unless we had to," Mrs. Barry said.

They explained what had happened.

Mrs. Barry then turned her attention to the carcass. She assigned Bill Dan and Letitia to strip off the lean meat and hang the strips high on the paloverde so that no ground creatures could get at it.

They cut the venison into pieces six to ten inches long. Soon they had filled a big crock. Bill Dan, with Letitia's help, strung the strips as high as he could reach, humming as he worked. He could tell that Letitia liked being with him. Her intimate tone and her casual manner showed it. In the meantime, Darrell Duppa, none too skilled with a knife, had left camp to do guard patrol again.

Roxie Webb and Leonti had left camp together after lunch to search for the special paloverde which Bill Dan and Darrell had been unable to find the previous day. Maybe, as Roxie had hoped, he and Leonti would return to camp with bags filled with nuggets of pure gold.

When they had reached the upper plateau and staked their horses, they separated after agreeing on emergency signals. The lay of the rugged plateau was such that they could stay in sight of each other for about an hour.

Moving silently, yet with a strange exhilaration, Roxie soon felt awed by the majesty of the red-rock mountain world, so vastly different from the piney woods of the Texas homeland that had been on his mind recently. Here were no tall, stately conifers, although a few needled pines did indeed grow in this high altitude. One cluster was at hand now. They assailed his senses not so much by appearance as by fragrance. "Be doggone!" he muttered, moving to touch them.

The growths had no central trunks, but were thick with limbs, which held many stubby branches, each heavy with clusters of short, stiff needles and small brown cones.

He poked at one of the cones with his rifle muzzle. A cascade of little brown "coffee beans" rattled out and tumbled through the foliage to the ground. Roxie picked up one of the beans and popped it into his mouth. It cracked easily and he sampled the tiny meat of the nut.

He smiled. "That's good. Tastes like pecans."

With a powerful hand he shook the tree hard and the brown nuts fell to the ground. He soon had a pocketful of them to take back with him.

He pushed on, humming, searching. As the two men had done the previous day, he found not one horse head on the cliffs, but several. One formation appeared like his mental image of Christ. He knew then that his brain was tricking him, and he suspected that Old Man Walz had been similarly tricked. Likely Mr. Walz had thought he had seen a horse head on these rock walls.

Roxie came onto Weaver's Needle as unexpectedly and dramatically as Bill Dan had said he would. It was as if the high plateau had been made into a gigantic outdoor theater. He paused to admire its majesty and to judge its size. That Mexican hat crown, that Needle, was well-named, for it stretched up into the sky. No wonder it was a sacred place to the Apaches. It looked like a temple even to him.

Now he must find that paloverde with the pointing arm. "It has to be around here some place," he said to himself.

He had felt Bill Dan's and Darrell's disappointment the night before when they had come in. They were experienced, sharp-eyed hunters, but they hadn't found it. Roxie had promised himself that he would surely track it down tomorrow. He hoped he would have that honor before Leonti did. Now this was tomorrow, and. . . .

The Superstition plateau was nine hundred times as big and wild and rugged as he had envisioned. Moreover, there were thousands of paloverdes. He searched unsuccessfully until hunger began to assail him. Guessing the time to be past eleven o'clock, he began to swing back toward their place for nooning, and soon came onto another one of those trickling mountain streams. He drank with pleasure, bathed his sweaty face and grimy hands and then pushed on.

Fifty yards farther, he stopped abruptly as he came upon another rock overhang. This one had eroded to make a deep oval cave at least thirty feet high. He couldn't be sure how far back into the mountain it went. But right at the entrance he saw a dozen or more large dark grey stones that had been hollowed out in the middle in a down curve. He was excited by the sight of them. He studied the area and found several smaller oval-shaped grey stones, one of which fitted into one of the hollowed-out pieces. "Grinding rocks for those pine nuts and mesquite beans," he said to himself. He could readily envision people kneeling and grinding a kind of meal at this spot. This was probably the site of an ancient village. He decided he should tell Leonti.

Moving at a half-trot, he hurried back up the slope until he could see the moving figure of his friend — a bare dot against the landscape — nearly a half mile away. He climbed up on a high boulder and started to wave his arms.

The answering wave came promptly; Leonti's eyes were alert and he came down, slipping sidewise and edging around thorny cacti. When Roxie showed him the grinding rocks, Leonti said they were common among Mexicans and Indians for grinding corn.

Roxie observed that the village site was almost hidden in an overgrowth of brush. Now, with Leonti at hand, he used his rifle to push some limbs aside as he moved up toward the cliff. In a moment he came to the main niche, the cavelike gash into the stone of the mountain. Here they found evidences of human habitation. The inner walls of the cave had pictures scratched on them, crude etchings of people and animals and weird geometric designs.

Roxie suddenly grinned, his handsome face shining with pleasure. "Leonti, my friend, red men have been here, but I'll bet I'm the first white man ever to see this place!" Roxie searched under the lip of the cave and poked his rifle through a pile of debris heaped against the rear wall. Suddenly he saw what unmistakably was the body of a human being. It seemed to be almost petrified and it certainly was not an Indian. The clothing, which was surprisingly well preserved, consisted of a shirt, a jacket, trousers, and shoes. Roxie almost panicked.

He and Leonti stood for a moment staring first at the corpse and then at each other. "Let's look around a little more and then report back to Bill Dan and the others," Leonti said.

"*Sí, señor.*" Leonti's face was serious.

Somewhat gingerly they poked their rifle muzzles

through the trash and soon found what each of them had been expecting. Five minutes later they were carrying a heavy burden back to their horses.

The trip back was uneventful, yet charged with expectancy. They were still half a mile from camp when they saw a moving figure, and they knew that Darrell Duppa had spotted them. Darrell was holding his rifle high, waving it with one hand in welcome. They knew he must have called to the others, for they, too, ran out and joined him, then all four started uphill.

"What luck?" Bill Dan cried eagerly, as the two groups met.

Neither Roxie nor Leonti spoke, but as they slowly reined up, they could see that Roxie's face was beaming. He reached behind him, straining a bit to lift a heavy bag.

11

Half Bushel of Ore

Bill Dan could see that his friends were close to exhaustion. Even their horses stood panting with their heads down, patiently waiting to be unsaddled and watered. Bill Dan stepped over to help Roxie dismount.

"Whoo," Roxie gasped, "that mountain drains a man's sap."

Leonti slid off his horse, Kino, and tossed the heavy bag to the ground.

"What is it?" Letitia asked.

Leonti didn't answer, so Mrs. Barry said, "You have found something. Is it ore? Gold?"

Bill Dan spoke. "You found it, I hope."

All of them knew he was referring to the mine.

There wasn't a sign of levity. Roxie's smile faded as the five people gathered in a half-circle around the blanket bag.

"Not the mine," Roxie said, "but — there's a dead man up there."

"*Si*," added Leonti. "A *Mexicano*. Is dry. Is old. Long time back. From Dan Miguel Peralta, his people. *¿No es verdad?*"

"Yes, I think so," Roxie agreed.

"Where did you find it, Roxie?" Letitia asked. "Was it a skeleton?"

"No skeleton, ma'am. A whole dead man. Old, dried up, back under a rock in a trash pile. It was a sort of cave."

The group stared at the bag almost as if they expected the corpse to be in it. Roxie made no move to open it. He began to elaborate on how he had discovered the ancient grinding stones and what appeared to be the site of an abandoned village. "Back in that cave in a pile of trash is where I found the dead man." he repeated. "I first saw a part of his shirt. I poked my rifle into the trash and pulled out a leather bag!"

"Another one!" Letitia exclaimed. "With ore in it?"

"It was dry — hard and crackly. I figured it might fall apart, so I broke a hole in it big enough to see the yellow gold. Then I wrapped it up. Here it is, yes, ma'am." He squatted on the ground to open the parcel. The motion of his horse as it had moved down the hill had broken the old leather into bits, as Roxie had anticipated. But around the pieces was a good half bushel of ore concentrates.

Bill Dan noticed immediately that these rocks were the same as those from the Peralta expedition. Only, the latest ones looked to be the richest of all the concentrates found.

"Not from the mine itself, then," he said, staring at the pile.

"No. Bill Dan, if there is a paloverde tree with just one arm up there, it sure is hidden. We couldn't find it anymore than you and Lord Duppa could. But when we go back. . . ."

It was a promise, an agreement shared by the men.

"I want to go," Letitia said firmly. "A woman often has to find a man's own shoes when they are right under his bed."

"I doubt whether you'd do any better than the boys," her mother said gently, "but go ahead. I'd like to go myself."

"All right, then you shall," Bill Dan said. "This party is as much yours as it is ours. And I hope you do find the paloverde landmark. It'll be worth your while just to see Weaver's Needle close up."

"That is a pure fact!" Roxie agreed, and Leonti nodded. "Hey, I've brought you something else, Letitia. And Miss Nannie, too, ma'am."

Roxie seemed to have forgotten his fatigue. He dug into three pockets of his jacket, and after asking Miss Nannie to sit down and spread out her apron, he poured about two quarts of pine nuts into it.

"*Piñones*," explained Leonti. "How you say it, Roxie *amigo*? The pine noots."

"Pine nuts, off a scrubby pine tree. But prettiest thing you ever did see, ma'am. It had a million little cones out of which these nuts came sprinkling down when I shook

129

the tree. They're for eating. Go on, everybody. Try one. They taste like pecans."

The nuts were a treat. Mrs. Barry said she would make Letitia shell them and then she would bake a nutcake for everyone.

The party then started back toward their camp. When they neared the campfire, Bill Dan ordered Roxie and Leonti to rest. "I'll feed the horses for you," he said. He gave each of the two horses a quart of corn which they had brought from Phoenix. Usually the animals were expected to feed on the grasses nearby, but today they had earned a treat. When he had finished, he ate quickly and then relieved Darrell of guard duty. Before Darrell started back to camp, Bill Dan told him about Roxie and Leonti's discovery. Darrell seemed more excited than the others, especially about finding the site of an old village.

"Yes, that must be an old Indian habitation," he said. "I want to study it. Likely it dates back three or four hundred years, maybe more. Similar villages have been found elsewhere. I'll write to an archaeologist friend about it."

Bill Dan was amused at Darrell's being more interested in archaeology than in gold. He smiled at Darrell. "Go in and eat," he said. "We'll go up there tomorrow to see it."

The Englishman lifted a hand in salute and started away. "I'll relieve you at midnight," he said. "Rox and Leonti need rest. Cheerio."

Bill Dan liked the idea of being alone under the stars. He felt no cause for worry, although he decided he would move around dutifully and keep a sharp lookout.

By ten o'clock a glow appeared behind the jaggered eastern rim of the mountains and soon it grew into a spot of fire. It grew bigger, rounded itself and became startling in size and brilliance.

After Lord Duppa had relieved him, Bill Dan slept soundly. He got up at dawn and quietly readied the horses. He caught the scent of an early fire. In a few moments Letitia came down the trail to the corral to join him. She had brought him coffee laced with molasses in a steaming tin cup. Neither spoke, but they smiled at each other in the early morning light. Bill Dan took the cup from her. "I appreciate this," he said. "I've saddled six horses so we can all go up there today."

"Oh, Bill Dan! Thanks."

She looked so pretty to Bill Dan that it hurt. He had to force himself to breathe deeply, then swallow the scalding coffee to keep from acting sentimental. "We'll take a shovel and a pick," he went on, "and we'll dig that poor soul a grave." He took her arm to walk her back to camp.

After they had eaten and tidied up their campsite, the party of six rode single-file up Peralta Canyon well before the sun had topped the peaks. Black shadows were fleeing fast down the slopes, fading into purple, then blue, and finally into nothingness. By the time they reached the first rest stop, the sun was intense. It was tempered to coldness, however, because of the altitude.

Roxie guided the group unerringly to the village site and the cave where he had found the corpse of the Mexican. Judging from the condition of the body, Darrell said that the man might have died during the intense summer heat; therefore, his body had become rocklike in a few weeks, as was often the case. Sandstorms would blow dirt and trash in a swirling fury and would cover, then uncover, the body several times.

"He must be from the Peralta expedition," the Englishman said. "Why he died up here instead of down on the flats is anyone's guess. He may have tried to get away on his own before Indians struck."

"How do you mean?" Bill Dan asked.

Darrell shrugged. "Maybe he simply grabbed that bagful of the richest nuggets and hightailed it, figuring that he would make his way back to Mexico alone."

"You think the bag has that much gold in it?"

"I can't say. I've already told you that I am no assayer. But from what little I know, I'd guess Roxie's find yesterday doubled our fortune."

After the men had dug a grave, Miss Nannie read the 46th Psalm and prayed for the man's soul.

After the brief ceremony, Letitia picked up a long pole and began to dig with it into the pile of trash at the spot inside the cave where the body had been found.

She managed to pull out strips of clothing that had rotted. She found an old canteen, too. It was empty, but still in good condition. She also found another leather pouch which at one time may have contained food. All six watched her with interest.

"I have a feeling that the man maybe got sick," Letitia said, "or perhaps he was bitten by a rattlesnake; then he crawled under this overhang and just plain died. He showed no Indian arrow, no scalping."

133

"That's as good a guess as any," said Bill Dan.

She continued to poke and push and search although she did not really know what she was looking for. After a minute they heard her gasp. She had to pull hard, and she raked out a second leather bag.

This bag seemed about as large at the one Roxie had found, and the leather on it was so brittle that it disintegrated when they tried to lift it. But it, too, held a pile of the richest-looking ore they had seen up to now.

"I be doggoned!" Roxie grumbled. "That dead man — I never looked deep enough!"

Bill Dan picked up the bag and began to reconstruct the scene. "I don't doubt he had them tied together across the back of his saddle for balance. He had a long trek back home, don't forget that."

"What happened to his horse?" Rox questioned.

"Most likely it became meat for mountain lions. If we hunted all around for days, we might find parts of the saddle; maybe we'd even find some bones."

"Look, look!" Letitia cried, pointing to the paintings on the cave's walls.

Her shout startled them; in fact, Bill Dan swung his rifle up but soon lowered it. He turned to Darrell hopefully for interpretation, for he was interested in the pictures.

"I couldn't begin to say what most of the pictures mean," Darrell insisted. "It's anybody's guess. We need an archeologist." He studied the pictures. "Here's one that obviously records the story of a successful hunt. Lions, deer. See the antlers?"

"They look like pictures that schoolchildren might have drawn," Letitia suggested.

"Some people think that Indians have childlike minds, but the American Indian is very intelligent. He's had every right to fight back when we invade his territory. His cruelties to us, I daresay, in the long run have totaled no more than our cruelties to him."

The others were startled at Darrell's explanation. It was a none-too-popular point of view, Bill Dan knew, for he had heard it before, and he had seen white men become indignant about it. So, in order to forestall a possible argument, he brought their attention back to the gold nuggets they had discovered.

"I figure half of this is mine," he remarked, straight-faced, as he hefted the two ore bags now lashed across his saddle skirt. "Enough to get hitched to that blonde woman with the yellow hair and the long, slim . . . ."

"You'd have to whip us first!" Roxie Webb warned him.

Because the burial and Darrell's intensive study of the old village site had consumed most of the day, Bill Dan suggested that they try not to locate the mine, but return to camp. So they collected as many artifacts and relics as they could find — shards, arrow points, two beautifully ornamental cooking bowls, six stone axes, and the prettiest of the grinding stones — and loaded them on their horses. It was awkward cargo to carry on horseback, but they managed. Letitia protected the bowls with grease-wood foliage and carried them in her lap.

On their way back it began to rain. It fell in giant

drops and caught them beyond protection of the cave-like overhangs. Soon the storm struck with a fury.

"Can't see Sam's ears in front of me!" Bill Dan shouted. He tried to squeeze down into his jacket collar and turn his hat brim down. Doing that didn't help; besides, he heard no answer. He began to feel cold, and he knew that his companions also were cold. Darrell Duppa was the only one to keep a rainproof slicker tied behind his saddle. Bill Dan couldn't see Darrell or his horse, but he knew that they were ahead.

Suddenly he thought about Letitia! She had no protection, not even a cover for her head. He kicked Sam, who showed indignation at this insult, and leaped forward down the slippery slope. When he came close to her, he took off his leather jacket to put it around her. But he was too late.

She was riding along calmly and in comparative comfort, huddled dry under a voluminous yellow slicker.

12

Darrell and Letitia

Bill Dan was annoyed when he saw Darrell's slicker on Letitia, for he realized that he should have thought about her comfort himself. The rain was so intense that at times he had to lean his head over the saddle horn to keep the water out of his nose. He did not even try to guide Sam, who stepped with caution along the slippery gravel and sloping rocks. Twice he skidded to his haunches, almost unseating Bill Dan. "C-A-R-E-F-U-L!" he shouted to those behind him. They were strung out single file and probably couldn't hear him. The rain was driving hard, but above its sound could be heard the volume of the

Thunder Gods beating their tom-toms among the cliffs and canyons.

The storm had hit with the force of a blacksmith's hammer and lasted about forty-five minutes. Then it stopped abruptly.

Bill Dan lifted his head and twisted around on his saddle to look at Letitia, who was riding behind him. "Just look yonder — the sun!"

For at least ten seconds the rumble in the northeastern sky bounced around the mountain vastness. Then the claps diminished gradually like a wounded lion groveling and slinking away. Bill Dan was soaked to the skin and shivering. He wanted nothing more than to reach home to start a fire so that he could dry out and get warm. "You, Sam," he addressed his horse, "don't get fast and careless, now that the sun's out again. Stop hurrying." At the same time he reached out and grabbed the bridle of Letitia's mare. It would have been risky if they had broken into a trot, because both horses were over-loaded.

Settling in on their return — preparing supper, checking their property, seeing to the horses which had been left hobbled to graze, and caring for the ones ridden — took nearly an hour. Bill Dan's first job had been to build the fire.

"Never have I appreciated the luxury of heat more than I do now," Letitia said through chattering teeth.

And she wasn't even wet, Bill Dan noted, except for her legs and feet; Darrell's slicker had covered her well. Darrell literally oozed water as he worked, but did not complain. Letitia warmed her hands, then quickly set about to help her mother find dry clothes for the men. Bill Dan noticed her thoughtfulness as he noticed almost everything else about her, and he admired her even more. Even though he was busy, he could not help wondering if she favored Darrell over him. He couldn't blame her if she did, Darrell was educated and refined. Darrell would make a mighty fine husband.

That thought darkened his spirits as he led Sam off to the corral. Allerdice, he ordered himself silently, keep quiet, this is no time for thinking about girls and courting. Even so, he grumbled all the way down the watery trail. It was one thing to order himself not to think about Letitia; it was another thing to obey. His worst times were at night. He'd lie in his bedroll thinking about Letitia; then he'd dream about her.

Dinner that night was tasty and warming meat stew, accompanied by big saucers of cooked dried peaches and plenty of hot coffee. Everyone ate heartily, then pitched it to clean up afterwards. They were tired from the afternoon's ride and the storm, despite the finding of additional treasure.

"More better we sleep," Leonti Soto suggested. It was well before eight o'clock by Darrell's huge silver watch. "This golt ores, they keep for tomorrow, eh? *Si.*"

They were up early the next morning. The air was close to freezing. Letitia, Bill Dan, and Roxie stood before the fire shivering and rubbing their hands. Their collars were turned up, but their faces were wreathed in smiles. Bill Dan felt that he had never been happier. When he

140

turned to help Mrs. Barry cut some slices of pork, she pushed him aside.

"You just visit with the other young folks," she said. "I can do this. It does me good to hear you all talking and laughing."

On impulse he leaned down quickly to kiss her on the forehead. He had never done such a thing before, but it seemed to please both of them. Their good spirits brightened even more when Leonti Soto joined them, smiling and rubbing his hands briskly. *"Buenas dias, amigos! ¿Como esta? ¿Muy bien, hey?"* Leonti's broad mustache seemed to widen when he smiled. *"Si,* like you speak him, Bill Dan, I feel good enough to climb a cactoos with wild cat under each arm! So?"

They all laughed and sat down to breakfast. The day was off to a great beginning. They were in a mood for good fellowship rather than for gold hunting.

Presently Bill Dan saw Mrs. Barry go to the young paloverde tree that stood about twenty feet in front of the kitchen area. With a small paring knife she cut a quarter-inch notch in the shiny green of the trunk. Then she counted the other notches. "I think it is now December 6," she said. "It's getting on into winter, but likely it won't get too cold. We haven't done too bad considering the ore we've found, but the Dutchman's Mine is as lost as it ever was."

"Darrell says we have enough gold nuggets for each one of us to get about a thousand dollars," she went on. "That first find was a godsend, and now this new treasure — it's more than Letitia and I ever figured to own at one time, isn't it, dear?"

"It surely is, Mother. Two thousand dollars!" She spoke with awe, but gazing afar and daydreaming.

The thought of the Lost Dutchman mine began to haunt all of them again. One way or another, everybody had managed to get muddy in yesterday's rain. Consequently, Mrs. Barry insisted that today she and Letitia would do laundry for everyone while Bill Dan and Darrell went back up the trail. The other two would stay back for guard duty.

Bill Dan and Darrell put ample food in their saddlebags and added two strong sacks. They wouldn't need canteens today for every canyon and gully would be running, and every rock depression would hold an icy pool of rain water. Because the air was clean and zestful, Bill Dan led off singing. "Beau-ti-ful dream-er-r-r-r, Come unto me-e-e," he drew the words out. Darrell picked up the melody, matching his tenor with Bill Dan's baritone. Sam snorted, and the two men laughed.

As before, they separated and searched out the high plateau areas that were eye level with the Needle. Sam and the other horse had to be staked far down the slope to graze, but the foot trail going up was pleasant enough. Superstition Mountain had no really muddy areas; there was too much slope and too much rocky drainage to keep the trail wet. The entire landscape was brilliant today; bright greens mingled with the reds and yellows of the rocks, which had been washed clean by the rain.

Bill Dan noticed a greater profusion of plants on this trail than he had seen on the first trek up. He stood on a

143

shoulder-high boulder to shade his eyes and study the panorama.

At the noontime meeting, neither Darrell nor Bill Dan had any new observations to report to one another, so they continued dutifully to work other high-altitude reaches in the afternoon, and by agreement went down the slope to their staked horses at four o'clock.

As they went down the trail toward the horses, Bill Dan caught a glimpse of motion on a ledge about fifty feet above him and to his right. Reacting by instinct, he swung the muzzle of his gun swiftly and dropped to minimize himself as a target. He did not need to worry. A huge, tawny mountain lion ambled to the ledge. It was a beautiful cat, and no doubt minding its own business, Bill Dan told himself. Yet he wanted something to show for his day on the trail, and a lion pelt could be valuable. He decided to risk a shot. Darrell would now be coming toward him at the moment, anyway.

The rifle shot sounded like a cannon, and it brought Darrell hurrying in alarm. Bill Dan blew out the barrel, reloaded, then calmly ambled over to where the animal had toppled and rolled down the slope below the cliff. The bullet had hit directly behind its ear.

"What is it?" Darrell called anxiously. "What'd you shoot at?"

Nose to tail tip, the mountain lion measured nearly eight feet. They guessed it weighed a good hundred and fifty pounds. Together they skinned it. Tawny, sleek, short-haired, graceful, it was a pretty beast. Bill Dan began to

feel ashamed that he had killed it. He wished he hadn't. He stood spread-legged holding the pelt and stared down at the bloody carcass. Well, it was done now, and no doubt the buzzards would be feasting before nightfall. He carried the pelt to the horses.

To his surprise and dismay, Sam would have no part of the pelt.

Bill Dan had thought that all he would have to do would be simply to tie it behind the saddle. But Sam's eyes doubled in size, the whites showing. He snorted loudly. Then he backed up and reared, making it clear that he'd have no part of the mountain lion.

Sam won out. Darrell's horse acted offended, too, but Darrell gave him a sharp cut across the rump with a switch which convinced him that he would have to carry the pelt. Nevertheless, he danced around and kept turning his head as he tried to see the horror tied over his rump.

Both men knew that horses hate mountain lions. The faintest scent panics them. A large lion could spring from ambush, land on a horse's neck, and break it in three seconds. Horses sense the danger instinctively. They managed to get the pelt home, and Letitia was delighted to have it for a wall hanging.

The air had turned balmier after they reached camp, and the family gathered in a happy mood around the supper fire. They ate plump topknot quail, tender and juicy. Trapping the quail had been an easy job for Letitia, although wringing their beautiful, dainty necks had not been. Soon the talk drifted to a personal plane, and Darrell Duppa told them about his life in England. He mentioned

146

that his monthly remittance check amounted to five hundred dollars. To the others that much money seemed incredible.

"Yes," Darrell continued, staring at the coals, "it is indeed considerable money. Some I have wasted; some I still have. More will be waiting for me when I return. My people are well-to-do. But I'll say this: all that I have, all that I may get hereafter, will go into our common fund, along with the gold we own."

Bill Dan was appalled. That remark had done it, for sure. It secured Darrell Duppa's case with Letitia Barry. She's be a fool not to choose a man like that, one who had riches as well as character and kindness. His own spirits hit bottom.

As leader of the party, he finally forced himself to speak. "No, we couldn't figure on that, Darrell. It wouldn't be fair. That's your own. Whatever you get from home . . ."

"Will go into the same pot," Darrell repeated firmly. "I told you before, you people are my family now."

"Lordy, maybe I ought to take and toss you into the bath hole down there," Bill Dan teased. "Now shut up, will you, and get yourself to bed."

"*Si, seguro, si.*" Leonti Soto added.

Miss Nannie spoke, "All of you are mighty fine men. Don't you ever talk like that again, Lord Darrell Duppa. You hear me?"

Miss Nannie's ultimatum made it seem like a good time to close the meeting, so of one accord they drifted off to their respective beds.

Bill Dan did not drop off to sleep instantly, as he usually did. He tossed and he lay thinking. He knew that he himself was not well educated, he was not refined, nor was he romantic. Even Leonti Soto had more schooling and polish than he had. So it would, of course, be right and proper for Letitia to . . . Even Roxie Webb had a girl back in Phoenix who trusted him. As soon as the mine was found, they could go back there, and Rox would marry Ellen and . . .

He turned to face the rock wall. Fantasies danced through his semiconsciousness, and it was almost midnight before he went to sleep.

13

Campfire Songfest

It wasn't Bill Dan's turn to go up the mountain again the next morning, yet he was restless and felt a sense of urgency. He decided the urgency was personal. He needed to locate that confounded mine, get whatever treasure possible out of it, and take Letitia Barry back to civilization and marry her before somebody else did.

While the women prepared breakfast, he busied himself by helping Darrell fill in the large map of Superstition which they had been adding to each day.

"You covered this area," Darrell said, as he pointed to the area they had covered in their search the day before, "and shot the mountain lion about here." He made an X. "I tramped over the portion to the west of that." His finger moved on. "Altogether we have searched this much territory up there."

Bill Dan nodded. "But we can't say how much more

remains. And we might go back over our old tracks and find what we missed the first time. Seems to me we might as well take our chances and all of us go back up there to look."

"Could be you are right." As he spoke, Darrell studied the sketches of outstanding peaks, ridges, cliff faces, canyons and cuts which they had encountered, and labeled some of them. Weaver's Needle was in the center. "All of us can't go today. That rain washed a lot of dirt into our bath pool, and the women say they have to hang the venison out another day or two to dry after the wetting it got. Also, two of the horses have loose shoes, which Roxie must fix. So, Bill Dan," he said, "why don't you and Leonti go today, while Rox and I stay here and get the camp back in shape. Then maybe tomorrow all of us could . . . ."

"No!" The word snapped out of Bill Dan's mouth before he realized it. He didn't want Darrell Duppa left at home. Letitia had referred to him as "noble." He couldn't blame the Englishman if he moved right in on that advantage. Maybe he had even planned it that way. With Rox out of camp on guard duty half the time, anything could happen. Duppa could give Letitia a strong sales talk, get her promise, and upset all his plans.

But then, maybe Letitia ought to have the chance to make a choice. Who was he, William Dan Allerdice, to dictate where her happiness lay? If she preferred Duppa, . . . No, that didn't make sense, either.

He was miserable and frustrated as he struggled between leadership and personal desires. He backtracked quickly. "Well, yes, maybe so. But you and Rox can claim a special day up there when you want to. Rox is the best one with horseshoeing. And if you want to shovel . . . ." He forced a smile.

So the matter stood. He and Leonti rode until they were sky-high again, then set themselves for another day of intensive searching.

It was not a happy day for Bill Dan, and he doubted whether he really looked with the care that he should have used. At any rate, neither he nor Leonti found anything encouraging. They tried to stay within a half mile of the Needle, because that's where Old Man Walz had said the mine lay. They had given up hope of finding the horsehead cliff, but they tried to scan every one of the thousands of paloverde trees. After a few hours, however, things tended to blur and fuse together and one tree looked like the next one.

Besides, the day was unreasonably cold. Bill Dan figured that for every ten feet they went up the mountain, the temperature dropped one degree.

Neither man had thought to put on extra clothing; the warmth of the campfire at breakfast had lulled them, and this was the first real cold snap. The recent rain had caused the soil to drain itself, and trickles of water had been oozing down all the slopes. Therefore, this morning every rock overhang was festooned with icicles which had turned silver and gold in the pale sunshine. They made the mountain more beautiful than ever, but the air made Bill Dan's nose and ears ache.

A warming sun helped to ease their suffering before

151

midafternoon; then the temperature again slipped below freezing. It made walking more tiring, so that by three o'clock the two men decided to head back home. When they finally reached their horses, they noticed that Sam's lower lip had tiny icicles hanging from it.

"You lazy old son of a gun," Bill Dan growled. "If you had kept on grazing, your mouth wouldn't have froze."

The two gold hunters had ridden only about a hundred yards when Bill Dan spotted a string of especially large icicles hanging within reach. On impulse he swung Sam over, stood in his stirrups, and reached to snap off one of the icicles.

"Ho, what you do, *amigo?*" Leonti's tone implied that his friend was slightly crazy.

"Souvenir for Letitia."

The icicle was more than six feet long and six inches thick at its heavy end. He snatched up handfuls of thick, greasewood foliage in which to cradle it across his saddle. Then he let Sam have free rein.

As he rode into camp with the icicle, grinning and feeling rather childish, he became fearful that Letitia might ridicule him. He wished he had had more sense than to act like a fourteen-year old.

Letitia didn't ridicule him at all. "Every gold camp should have a pet icicle in its duffel" she said, smiling. "Thank you, kind sir. I judge you found nothing else?"

They were tired, and everybody knew that if they had found the mine, or even the paloverde with the pointing arm, the mood would have been entirely different. Roxie

152

took the horses to the corral, while the searchers sat cross-legged before the fire and sipped coffee.

Nothing more was accomplished during the next few days. Twice all six went up into the mountain and scanned the region around Weaver's Needle with eagle eyes, but without results. Strangely enough, however, no one admitted disappointment or discouragement. Bill Dan spoke of this to Letitia one night after supper, when chance gave them some privacy down near the stream.

"Oh, Bill Dan," she said, "how could we be depressed? We'll find the mine yet, and in the meantime, it's wonderful just to live up here!"

He smiled slowly, absorbing what she had said. Letitia was given to enthusiasm, he knew. It was wonderful, for sure, to live up here — mainly because of her. He worshiped her, but couldn't say so, not here, not now.

"I know what you mean," he managed. "Guess I feel the same way. A body has to live somewhere. Can't think when or where I've had better living."

"That's exactly what I mean."

Bill Dan knew, however, that it couldn't go on forever. True, there hadn't been a hint of Apaches, and the family might live here until spring on wild game and foodstuffs they had brought with them. But it would be risky.

The peaceful mood and the good feeling seemed to have suffused all of them that evening. For once Bill Dan ruled that they didn't need a guard, at least for about two hours, so that everybody could sit around the fire and enjoy the warmth.

Mrs. Barry smiled. "This is the time to bring out the sack of popcorn that Adaline Gray gave me," she said. "Tisha, get the big skillet, put salt and a spoonful of lard in it, and bring the cover."

Bill Dan was happy; happy enough even to sit beside Darrell, his friend and rival; happy to see Leonti Soto's smiling eyes; happy when Roxie Webb began to do a few simple magic tricks. Roxie could put a pebble under three little old seashells he carried, wiggle them around, and you could never guess which shell the pebble was under.

It turned into a real good party, better than any church sociable Bill Dan ever remembered attending. He caught himself laughing often. When urged to tell a story, he responded with a yarn about Daniel Boone, who could choke a bear to death with his bare hands; then another one about the French pirate named John Lafitte. He said John buried his treasure near a lake in East Texas.

"Gold?" Darrell Duppa asked, smiling.

"That's what they say," Bill Dan answered, "though nobody could ever find hide nor hair of it. No more than we can find ours."

Leonti brought out his guitar and tuned it while walking back to the fire. Without invitation he broke into a song about Dixie.

Bill Dan looked around. "I wonder whether these old cliffs ever heard such as this before." Privately he figured this was surely the happiest night of his life, especially when Letitia settled down on her lion skin beside him.

154

Then she got up, refolded the skin, and gave him half to sit on. Her shoulder touched his and his sensitive nose again caught her subtle, indefinable fragrance. It sent his blood racing, although he forced himself to remain calm.

While Miss Nannie sang some hymns in a low voice, he told himself that he must do something soon about her daughter. A man couldn't drift on like this, wanting and yearning and losing sleep at night. If only they'd found the gold mine. With his share, he could have gone to town, shaved and bathed and bought new clothes and even got a haircut. Then he could call formally on Letitia and present his proposal. That was the way it should be done. But he was reluctant to depend on that mine. He didn't doubt that they'd find it sooner or later, but now time was being wasted. If he aimed to cut out Lord Duppa, he'd have to do it soon.

His thoughts crystallized another idea that had been growing in his mind for a week. Silently his thoughts drifted back to his last visit with Old Man Walz. He reviewed everything Darrell had said about the Peraltas. There had to be a mine here. Plainly, it had already been worked. He shut his eyes and envisioned the four hundred Mexicans encamped on the other side of Superstition; he tried to project himself into whatever they most likely had done. He didn't reach a conclusion because Letitia Barry nudged him.

"You're asleep!" she said. "It's time to end the party."

He blushed, then grinned and apologized. "Sorry. I wasn't asleep. I just had my eyes shut, thinking."

Darrell produced his silver watch and said it was eleven o'clock, so Bill Dan stood up immediately. "Is it that late? Ah, well." He felt guilty, because for the first time, and for a longer time than he had intended, he hadn't kept a guard out.

He wrapped his heaviest clothes around him and picked up his rifle. He would stand guard until dawn. Miss Nannie wrapped a scarf around his neck, then tied it over his head and ears and put his hat on top.

"No, ma'am, just put the scarf around my neck," he said. "I have to keep my ears open to hear, whether it's cold or not. And no gloves, please. I need my trigger finger ready."

He told himself that he had on enough clothes to keep an army warm, but the night air penetrated to his bones. He moved the neck cloth up around his nose. It was running a little, and two tiny icicles formed just as they had on Sam's lip. In spite of his discomfort, he smiled at the thought, and moved silently as he scanned the wilderness. Somewhere, far off, a coyote howled.

He shrugged and inhaled deeply of the cold, thin air; then he stretched his free arm high and walked on silently. He needed the exercise. Soon he reverted to his thoughts about the Peralta expedition. An idea was beginning to grow in his mind, and it grew stronger and stronger.

He gave up the idea after a while and started to plan for the next day. He was the family leader, so he always needed to be prepared. Soon it would be dawn. He'd go in, breakfast, get the others squared away for the day, then plunge into his blankets and sleep.

That would bring the time close to supper, he reckoned, and he smiled gently. They'd have to give themselves another party some night soon.

14

The Mystery Ride

Bill Dan was still groggy at breakfast, so Roxie Webb took command and made plans as he downed his fourth cup of coffee. "All right," he said, "we have voted, and it is unanimous. We'll all go back to hunt for the mine today except for Bill Dan. He'll stay here and have supper ready for us when we get back."

The others nodded emphatically. Leonti Soto said, "*Si,* he sleep all day. Hide in cave. Hah, nothing bother him. Is loafer."

After the others had gone. Bill Dan crawled under a rock, choosing a hidden place about two hundred yards distant in case there was any danger. He had barely rolled into the blankets before he fell asleep.

A clap of thunder jolted him awake. Before his sensibilities returned, he had rolled several feet, clutching his rifle ready to shoot. His ears were ringing, but he could see nothing except a few streaks of rain. A second clap of thunder put him into action. He hastened back to his bed, put on his shoes, trotted down a slope and around a curve to the home camp, where he put on his slicker and hastened to build up the fire which had dropped into coals under four inches of ashes.

The rain lasted for ten minutes, then it turned to sleet. Bill Dan studied the leaden sky and tried to guess what time it might be. With no sun or stars to guide him, it could be noon or four o'clock. His stomach suggested that it could be eight o'clock, so he set about cooking supper as Roxie had ordered.

In another hour the others arrived. They were wet as ducks, despite the rainproofs they wore. Letitia noticed his questioning look as she swung off her mare.

"The rain caught us when we were on foot away from the saddles. We never dreamed it would rain. The sky was so clear." She was shivering.

He led her straight to the fire, which had begun to die down into radiant coals. He found a patchwork quilt, warmed it, then wrapped it around her. He got one for her mother, too. The others came up. They were shaking with cold and squatted down beside the fire. Their clothing soon began to steam.

Bill Dan reached for the big pot of coffee. Each one took the scalding liquid gratefully, and Bill Dan joined them. Gradually, as the thaw set in, their good spirits returned. "The mountain she is big," Leonti said. "Is full with the *oro*, the gold, but who can find him?"

It was the only reference to another day of frustrating search. Bill Dan asked no questions.

His cooking wasn't Miss Nannie's, but it tasted good and it warmed the innards. Letitia hadn't been the only trapper. Nearly two weeks before, Roxie had rigged a trap of his own near the stream in what he thought was a rabbit run. Consequently, Bill Dan was able to make rabbit stew with onions and potatoes and dumplings. He gave each one a handful of raisins for dessert. Bill Dan munched his own portion of raisins contentedly as he leaned back against a log section which he had dragged close to the warmth. "I have something to tell you," he said.

"What is it, Bill Dan?" Letitia asked. Her face seemed pinched with fatigue.

"Well, I've been studying about all this," he said, waving his arm in an arc that indicated the mountain. "You know, the mine and those Mexicans, the ore concentrates, the Indian attack, and all."

The others nodded.

"Sam and I are rested. I will stand guard until midnight, then wake Leonti for duty, and you, Darrell, can relieve him later. And if you all don't mind, I'll wake Roxie and ask him to come out with me at midnight. I mean, if Rox . . ."

"Where to? May I go?" Letitia interrupted.

"No, ma'am, please." He wasn't teasing and he didn't smile. "Hope you others will stay here and. . . . You can all go on up the hill again and look some more if you want to, but stay together and keep a sharp lookout for Apaches."

"Where do you and Rox aim to go?"

161

"Can't say exactly; it's just an idea. But we may not be back for two or three days. All right?"

"Not on your tintype, Bill Dan Allerdice!" Letitia spoke up. "Why don't we all go, if you have something special in mind?"

He shook his head, but he avoided her eyes. "Nothing so special, nothing at all for sure. It's just that.... Well, we aren't getting anywhere hunting for that paloverde with one arm. So I been thinking...."

He refused to be specific, but eventually he had his way. They were too fatigued to argue. Privately he told Roxie that their horses, bedrolls, slickers, canteens, food, and other equipment would be ready. Roxie seemed pleased to be the one chosen, and he hurried off to get some sleep.

Out on night patrol, Bill Dan at first had to creep along in the intense darkness. But soon it began to lighten. He studied the sky. Yes, sir, yonder over that stretch of peaks was a patch with four stars in it where clouds were fleeing like disturbed sheep trying to settle down for the night. Likely it would soon be fair.

Soon it was fair. He marveled at Arizona weather. Back home in Texas, a rainy spell was likely to last weeks and be clammy and cold between. Out here, the thunder shook a man's liver and turned him gray-headed. It rained on him ten minutes, then there were no clouds for maybe a month. He gazed up toward Four Peaks where the Apaches were said to live and saw the last of the clouds fading. He felt good; he was a bit cold, but he was in fine spirits.

Almost silently he put Leonti on guard duty, speaking briefly to him and, for some reason, shaking hands with him. Then he and Roxie mounted their horses. Sam swung unbidden uphill, and Bill Dan had to knee him to reverse. The animal paused, twisted his head around to look inquiringly, but obediently changed directions.

"So we're not going up Peralta Canyon," Roxie murmured.

"No."

There was a pause. "What's on your mind?" Roxie asked.

Bill Dan did not reply, but guided Sam southwestward and downward onto a flat of decomposed granite. Roxie moved alongside.

"Not exactly sure myself. It's just that I have been thinking a lot this past week."

"About what?"

"Nothing you could hitch a horse to." Bill Dan paused while the horses adjusted themselves to a fast walk. "It's just that you all made me the leader. I feel responsible."

"Sure, but I still . . . ."

"Well, we haven't been able to locate that confounded mine, and weeks keep passing, and . . . ."

Roxie turned to him. "Hold on! You ain't thinking about going back to Phoenix? Maybe to find us a house again? Now you just wait! We have to ask the others if we . . . ."

"I never said anything about going back to Phoenix. I just said I've had a thought that won't give up nagging me, but I'm not sure of what we can do. So I asked you to go with me. I'd rather not say yet what it's all about. But I do need to talk up to it, Rox."

"You could have brought Lord Duppa. He's smarter than me."

"No, that's just what I didn't want. In the first place, you and I are Southerners. We can read each other's minds; we trust each other."

"Sure. Yes." Roxie didn't probe the matter; he simply waited.

"But Duppa's part of what I have on my mind," Bill Dan said.

The horses' hoofs were making soft squashy sounds in the sand. Neither man felt any fear. There'd be no reason to think that an Indian would be out on a freezing night like this.

"I needed to let her stay with those other two while I'm gone," Bill Dan said.

Roxie knew who the "her" was, but he remained silent.

"We'd better circle," Bill Dan interpolated, as he looked up and around. "We have to swing north, anyway. I needed to let her stay close to them for a while so that she could make up her mind."

Roxie followed Bill Dan's thinking, but he didn't agree. "Me, I'd move right in there, man," he said. "You take Ellen, she had four or five fellows. But like I told you before, I stepped right up front, swung a few fists, made those guys light a . . . ."

Bill Dan lifted his hand and waved it from side to

side. "No. That's all right for you. Make Ellen proud of you. She even told Letitia as much. But me. . . ."

"She did? She told Letitia?"

"She sure did." Bill Dan chuckled. "You've got Ellen Austin sewed up in a bag. She'll wait for you. But in my case . . . ."

"Let's go home, Bill Dan. Let's take off right now and ride on in to Phoenix. What's forty miles? We can make it before sundown. I'll marry up with Ellen, get us some fresh groceries, buy her a horse, and all three of us come on back out here . . . ."

"Keep quiet. Look who's talking. A minute ago you bawled me out when you thought I wanted to go to town. No, we don't need to go to Phoenix yet. But I need to let Letitia expose herself to Leonti Soto, and especially to Darrell Duppa, and also to work out some thinking in her own way."

"You could whip either one of them, even both at once. You could do it with one hand tied behind your back!"

"Bunk! And you know it. Anyhow, I wouldn't. I mean I wouldn't want to get Tisha that way. Her case is different from Ellen's, and you are different from me. I want Tisha to see everything there is good in those other two, then choose me, see? Maybe I'm crazy, but . . . ." He finished with a shrug.

"Yes, sir, you sure are," Roxie assured his friend. "But you're you, and if that's the way you want it, then all right."

"Darrell even wrote her a poem."

"Yeh. Pretty, too. Girls like poems. How are you going to talk when you propose to her?"

Bill Dan shot him a look of contempt. He didn't answer, but he wondered what he would say. Finally he spoke with great seriousness. "I could say, 'Miss Letitia, ma'am, you know all about me, but could I maybe possibly hope that you might consent to honor me by becoming my wife. I would be mighty proud, ma'am. . . .' How would that do, Rox?"

Rox managed not to grin. "You have to say something about love. Women like that. So when you propose, you say what you just said — that's real good — but first you get on one knee and say something about love, stuff like that. They have to have that."

"Um. Well, but . . . ." It was a fearful prospect, yet Bill Dan faced it as an inevitability. His lips even now were set firm. He stared straight ahead, forgetting to scan the horizon for Indians. "That Duppa, *he* could talk mush, I vow. Likely he will."

Roxie chuckled. "Trouble is, you like him. You and him are good friends."

"Yes, for a fact I do. I hate to be against him in this. And Letitia likes his speech. I heard her say so. Me, I talk like a clod."

"That don't cut no ice, man. Get your tail out from between your legs; defend yourself. You hear me?"

The two horses were moving faster, heads bobbing rhythmically. Bill Dan forced himself to refocus on the matters at hand. They had been riding in a great arc since leaving camp. First they swung south, then west, crossing a mesa-like upthrust and moving through a landscape that held fewer of the giant saguaros and more of the lacy paloverde, mesquite and ironwood trees. Many dangerous chollas and catclaw bushes covered the ground. The barrel cacti looked like young saguaros, serrated and bristling with thorns. The barrels provided a kind of compass, Bill Dan had learned, because they seemed always to lean south. Also, he had been told that if a body were dying of thirst, he could chop into one and obtain at least a quart of drinkable water.

"Say, we're back close to where that Mexican party was hit by the Indians. Right? The Peraltas?" Roxie broke the silence.

"Yes," agreed Bill Dan. "Right in here, where we first found their sign and some of the concentrated ore."

"How come we come back here?"

"Well," Bill Dan replied after a pause, "it's a sort of feeling inside me. I know that doesn't make sense, but . . . ."

"How far?" Rox asked presently.

"Can't say for sure. Likely, not far enough to be seen. I don't think any Apache scouts have reason to come down to these flats this time of year. We faced more danger when we first came from Phoenix. Lord Duppa says they ride down mostly after harvest season. They raid the valley Indians, take their crops if they can. That'd be more like October. This is getting close to Christmas."

"Christmas! A fact, doggone if it ain't! And I promised Ellen . . . ."

"Promised her you'd be back by then?"

Bill Dan knew that they all had to locate and work

the mine and be back in Phoenix in time to celebrate Christmas. The time had come to tell Roxie his plans. "But if I tell him," he mused silently, "he'll think I am crazy. Couldn't blame him."

An hour passed, then two, then three. He called a halt and both he and Roxie dismounted. The air was stinging, though not damp. Funny how it could rain hard, then an hour later, the air would feel as dry as toast.

Sam shook his saddle as well as himself, grunted, then stretched low to crop a tall bunch of grass.

"Slip off bridles, and neck-rein them, shall we?" Bill Dan suggested. "The stars and the moon make enough light to graze by, but not enough for Indians to see us from any distance. Do us all good to rest a spell. You hungry?"

"I could eat something."

From Sam's saddlebags Bill Dan took out two huge biscuits left over from breakfast the day before, which were wrapped in clean greasewood foliage. Between the slices were generous pieces of meat seasoned with pickles. No food ever tasted better, they decided, as they sat on the cold ground enjoying the sandwiches. As a treat, Roxie added a handful of piñon nuts for each of them.

Presently Bill Dan buried the greasewood wrapping under a bush, no sense leaving telltale signs when you don't have to. He hoped another shower would come soon and erase their tracks. Though the air was penetrating, the two men hugged themselves close and lay back to back on the grassiest spot they could find. They rested for nearly an hour; then they resumed their ride.

"I'm pointing us back toward Superstition," Bill Dan

explained. "Only the north side this time. It's the Indian side, but as I said, we won't likely have trouble here in winter. The thing is, this is probably the side by which those Peralta Mexicans went in. It looks like the easiest approach, and they wouldn't have known about the Apache strongholds up this way toward those Four Peaks."

"Yes," agreed Roxie.

"We did know, thanks to Darrell, so we swung south to put the mountain between them and us. If you want to go back, you can. But I've been nursing this feeling inside me for days, and I wanted you to come with me."

He hadn't meant to coerce Roxie; but suddenly he realized that no force on earth could make his friend turn back. So both rode steadily, pointing directly at the distant snow-covered Four Peaks, which looked as if they wore a mantilla of old Spanish lace.

"You're looking for something extra special?" said Roxie.

"Yes," replied Bill Dan.

15

Mexican Treasure

Always considerate of the horses, Bill Dan stopped twice to feed and rest them, then they pushed on quickly, though cautiously, looking like ants crawling up the vast north apron of the mountain. They kept to the thickest growths so that they were hidden, then they zigzagged among the massive boulders.

"What are we looking for?" Roxie pressed Bill Dan for an answer.

"A cave entrance. One that would be easy to reach with horses. Not the one way up in the mountain canyons, but one close to the base here, most likely."

When they came upon a stream, they following its lively trickle uphill, around rocks and crevasses until they found its source overflowing a basin perhaps ten feet across and twice as deep. It would have been a godsend to an expedition of four hundred men and animals.

Within a few minutes, they again discovered the blackened rock walls and ceilings of long-forgotten campfires. Bill Dan felt his heart quickening. Before another quarter hour passed, he guided Sam through a heavy mountain forest banked at a cliff base. He reined Sam up silently. Before him yawned the black mouth of a cavern in the face of Superstition Mountain.

It was no more than a hundred yards from the stream and was eroded out of soft granite that had been a part of the great bulk of the mountain. Bill Dan lifted his hand to halt Roxie, who was behind him. Wordlessly, both men swung down from their saddles and dropped their reins. Bill Dan, with rifle in hand, led the way into the cave to investigate.

The aperture was a gash about sixty feet deep and was singularly clean. The winds of time evidently did a good housekeeping job; no rain could enter, and the pileup of trash usual in such places was missing. Abundant daylight slanted in above the trees.

After almost trotting eagerly for several steps, Bill Dan stopped and pointed. "Holy day, Rox, I knew it! I just knew it!"

He put his rifle down and stooped to push his bare hands into a stack of old leather bags like those they had found before. He lifted one, then gently replaced it. His hands were covered with dust, but he ignored it. He pulled open the top of the bag, peered in, and saw what he had expected. "This cave was their headquarters," he said. "It has to be! I kept thinking about it."

Roxie, for a moment hypnotized, soon started to count. "Twenty-six more bags! Bill-l-l-l Dan!"

"It's plain that this was where Don Miguel Peralta stored the bulk of his concentrated ore. If they brought three or four hundred men here as Darrell said, then it stands to reason they located the mine and took out the richest ore they could find. Tons of it! They had the man-power and the pack animals. It's likely they had a trail right up to it, so that even the horses could travel."

"Right, right!" Roxie's spirits were high.

"Rox, they wouldn't have had any idea how much they had smelted down. There was no way to know. They had no scales for weighing."

"They took out more'n they could carry home."

"Likely. We would, too."

"Sure, sure, and they kept melting down that ore and stuffing little molded pieces into these bags!"

"Maybe they panicked and didn't take time to take away all their bags," Bill Dan said. "Maybe they figured to hightail it home with just what they had close at hand down there on the flats. Then they'd come back later with soldiers as guards to get the rest. But the massacre down yonder — the place is hardly six miles away. . . ."

"Exactly!" Rox nodded.

"All right, so let's do what they never had another chance to do. Get that big deerskin behind my saddle, two extra spreads of canvas, and some small lengths of rope. Now if we . . . ."

"Sure. Bags. But look here, Bill Dan. This stuff —

173

man, there's a load of it!" Roxie put his two hands under one of the dusty bags and hefted it. "It must weigh thirty, maybe forty pounds. We got only two horses."

Bill Dan was already moving fast toward Sam. "I was thinking . . . . you saw that old dead saguaro cactus back there just a few yards? Its dry ribs are strung out on the ground. You saw it?"

"I saw it. Sure."

"Those ribs are tough and hard and stronger than any green saplings. Darrell told us once how the Maricopas used them to make a travois behind a horse; you know — a long pole on each side like buggy shafts, the other ends dragging the ground, and a packload of stuff tied to the middle just behind the horse's tail. Remember?"

"Yeah," Roxie nodded. "You get the canvas and the ropes. I'll bring the poles. They're small; we'll need two on a side, maybe three, so they should be stout. Man, we've got ourselves gold!"

It took them the better part of two hours to fashion and load a travois for each horse. Poles had to be tied together, then cross-braced. The quarter-inch rope had to be woven into a kind of net, which, in turn, would hold the canvas or the deerskin on which the old sacks of ore concentrates were to be placed. The sack leather, as they had expected, was hard and brittle with age. They had to handle it with caution or the contents would spill out. Bill Dan cushioned the bags in a nest of the same grease-wood foliage that was often useful and usually at hand. He covered the bags with stronger mesquite limbs criss-crossed, then lashed everything to the poles.

The interval in preparing the travois gave the horses an opportunity to graze and rest, so that by four o'clock both of them were half asleep. The two men filled the canteens and stopped long enough to eat more of the food they had brought. Bill Dan was elated that his hunch had paid off. They had faced no trouble so far. They loaded thirteen bags of rich ore on the travois behind each horse. Now they would go back to their friends, a figurative wildcat under each arm, as Bill Dan had promised.

By six o'clock, when the sun was a mere band of gold on the horizon toward Phoenix, they mounted their horses. Sam took a step or two, then stopped, laid his ears back, turned his head, and snorted.

"Steady, Sam. Steady," Bill Dan said.

Sam snorted again. It was obvious that he resented pulling the travois. He was a saddle horse, aristocratic and proud. Only old scrub horses pulled things.

Bill Dan coaxed Sam, and Roxie coaxed his horse, Jody. Then, after a few sundry sidesteppings and snortings, the horses, with their riders and trailers, moved on.

Because the stars were so bright, they were able to travel until almost midnight. Bill Dan staked the horses so they could graze; then he hid himself in the shadows on a hillock a few dozen yards away to stand watch. After three hours, he awakened Roxie and took his turn to sleep. Both men knew that the sun wouldn't appear over Superstition until well after eight o'clock, but they could hardly wait to get back to camp to show their treasure. Probably they would all start back to Phoenix that same day. Bill Dan allowed himself a fleeting hope that maybe he could figure a way to convince Letitia to marry him.

Right now he had to lead Sam to pick the best "buggy" trail, for Sam, conditioned to more freedom, had his own ideas. Nevertheless, the travois slid safely along and they allowed themselves to daydream. Bill Dan talked about marriage and tried to improve the proposal he planned to make to Letitia, providing, of course, that Darrell or Leonti hadn't already sold themselves as her suitor.

Swinging around the south side of the mountain, they paused down the farther slope for rest and a cold breakfast. Roxie walked a short distance away from Bill Dan. Suddenly he yelled, "Bill Dan!"

The tone held a note of alarm. Bill Dan raised his rifle to belt position as he turned and ran toward his friend. "What's happened?" He followed Roxie's gaze and saw twin spirals of black smoke in the direction of their camp. "Two of them!" he said. "Two spirals! It's just getting light enough to see them!"

"Must have been burning some time to smoke up that high," Roxie said.

The message was clear. Bill Dan's mind raced. "It means they've left home. They're fleeing."

"Indians!" Roxie muttered scornfully. "And with us gone. Our people are bound to be coming back toward Phoenix. They're heading this way right now. It's the only place they could head for."

"We'll cut them off," Bill Dan said. "We'll build a signal fire of our own! One fire, one smoke, means to come in, remember?"

"Sure, but won't the Apaches see it? Our people might even think it's an Indian fire!"

"That's a chance we have to take, but it's worth trying." Bill Dan hesitated. "On the other hand," he said, "if we don't signal, we can be sure our folks will come hunting for us first. They'd never duck tail and leave us out here alone."

"That's true," Roxie said. "All right, a fire, and quick."

It took perhaps ten minutes to collect twigs, dry leaves and limbs from the undersides of trees and to pile them shoulder high. On top they placed a mass of greenery to produce the black smoke.

After they had lighted the kindling, they separated, each one going about four hundred yards in different directions to search for signs of their fleeing friends. Within half an hour, Bill Dan caught the sign — a low puff of dust, maybe a mile away. He couldn't spur Sam to race toward it, but he let him drag the travois at a trot. He beckoned to Roxie, swinging his arm in a long curve.

When they were half a mile from the smoke, they deployed again and hid themselves. Watching with great care, Roxie soon spotted Letitia on horseback, leading the other members of the family at a gallop.

"All right!" he yelled to Bill Dan. "It's them!"

There was a brief reunion, unemotional in tone, except for the concern for their survival. The party of six then turned toward Phoenix, moving their horses at a slow gallop.

"Darrell saw them first!" Letitia said rapidly. "There were two Indians, and maybe there were more not far behind. One was up the canyon as an out guard. We saw him at the first sign of dawn. Oh, Darrell!" She turned to him, and even in this moment of stress, Bill Dan could not help observing how much she worshiped the Englishman.

Darrell spoke grimly. "That's right. They finally got onto us, Bill Dan — two young Apaches who couldn't have been half a mile away. I know they saw me, too. They fled, and I fled, but we can be sure they'll bring all the help they can muster and come after us. No doubt they planned to attack us in our camp."

"Yes," Bill Dan answered. The thought was sobering.

Darrell continued, "In your absence, I decided we'd better get out of there fast and try to find you and Rox. Where have you been?"

"In the mountain," Bill Dan said. "We have gold. More concentrates. We're rich! I wish you could have brought the wagon."

Darrell shook his head. "Too slow and risky," he said. "I had no idea how much time we'd have. Still don't. But I figure it'll take a while for those two scouts to get back to their band and start on the trail after us. Praise God, we have a headstart."

"They'll know shortcuts," Bill Dan said. "Good thing you moved fast. I'm glad we're together."

Being reunited gave the members of the group new

courage. Six rifles could stand off many attackers who had only bows and arrows. The Indians might have one or two guns, but they were rarely accurate in using them.

"The horses are fresh," Bill Dan summarized the situation. "Canteens are filled. We have enough food. Let's press on to Phoenix. Forty miles is a powerful stretch for one day, but we don't have the wagon to slow us down. Besides, we have extra mounts if we need to change off. With luck, we could reach Phoenix late tonight."

"Would we have to go all the way today to be safe?" Letitia asked. "If we got within five or six miles. . . . ?"

"That's a thought," Bill Dan said. He turned to Leonti. "Since you're the lightest," he said, "you could take the fastest horse we have and race ahead to Phoenix and get help."

They decided to change the travel pattern. Hastily they rewrapped the bags of gold in blankets and bags and distributed them on the backs of six of the horses, behind the riders. Then once more, they moved westward. At first, Bill Dan dropped back. Then he realized that he could do nothing as a lone guard, so he rejoined the others. He made a special effort to comfort Miss Nannie, although she was sitting her saddle erect and calm.

At the appointed time, Leonti switched to a fresher horse. "See you in town, *amigos*," he said as he waved and smiled. "*¡Vaya con Dios!*" Then he pulled away from the others.

"There's five of us now," Bill Dan said to Letitia. "If worse comes to worst, you and your mother throw the

180

gold sacks off your horses and ride for Phoenix as hard as you can."

Common sense told him that the danger behind them would soon be approaching. Even if the Indians had nothing but bows and arrows, there'd be a good chance for somebody in the party to be killed.

That thought made him realize more than ever before how deeply he had come to love all these people.

16

Flight Through the Wilderness

Bill Dan reproached himself for not making everyone dump the heavy sacks of gold so that their horses could travel faster. Twice he called brief rest periods so that the horses could nip grass and suck up a few mouthfuls of water. He made the others eat, too, to keep up their energies. After the second rest period, he decided he'd cut back half a mile to look around.

He had gone barely quarter of a mile when he spotted the unmistakeable rise of dust not far behind them. He made a quick appraisal and then stood high in his stirrups. Twenty or thirty of them at least, he estimated as he kneed Sam around.

Bill Dan leaned low over his horse's neck and raced toward the group. They saw him coming and instantly they recognized his signal to flee. "I'll cut the extra horses loose!" he shouted. "Let them take their chances."

They took a wild plunge across the semidesert, an area now comparatively open and free of the dangerous cacti. Where they encountered greasewood bushes, they leaped over them. Every one of them was a skilled rider and fortunately the ore on their horses was tied securely.

At twilight they saw a peculiar red ball of "cloud" against the last waning glow of the sun. "That has to be help!" Bill Dan shouted.

"Please, God!" Letitia Barry called out.

Their faces were grim. Bill Dan was the only one to twist in his saddle to glance backward, but he could see no gain by the Indians.

The meeting with the people from Phoenix was effected with a minimum of words and no special drama. From a distance of two hundred yards or so, Bill Dan recognized the welcomed sight of Leonti Soto, who was returning as guide on a fresh horse. Leonti waved a greeting, then swung his arm in a big arc as he reversed his mount.

There were shouts, bits of laughter, and a few scattered words, but no real conversation. Of one accord, the little group of those fleeing merged with the larger group of rescuers, and all galloped again to the westward.

They forded Salt River, which was only about a foot deep and fifty yards wide. They allowed their horses to drink short drinks, then they spurred them on. Although it was no real barrier, the river spelled home and safety. The riders began to relax and to look behind them in defiance. Bill Dan knew that the danger was over. He glanced at Miss Nannie, who, with eyes closed, was moving her lips, as she still swayed gracefully on her horse. She looked tired, yet she appeared indestructible, so that Bill Dan's respect for her soared higher than ever. He also reached out to touch his friend Roxie Webb. He merely nodded, that was message enough. Darrell saw the gesture and lifted his hand. Everyone knew that Mrs. Barry was whispering a prayer of gratitude. Slowly, as of one accord, the men removed their hats until she had finished and opened her eyes.

A few moments later, Letitia, unsmiling but definitely expressing her own deep feelings, began to sing, *"Beau-ti-ful dream-m-mer, Come unto me-e-eeee!"* Although neither a hymn nor a great song, it carried a message that everyone understood. A second voice blended with hers, then all joined in.

Bill Dan had to swallow hard, for something was crowding his throat. Although he was dead tired, bleary-eyed, hungry, sleepy, and dirty, he had never felt so good in all his life.

Bill Dan was able to "let go" for the first time in days. They had moved back into the adobe house which they had formerly used in Phoenix. In fact, Mrs. Gray and the preacher's wife had cleaned it for them, had laid in a supply of groceries, besides wood for the stove and clean bedclothes.

"People are proud that all of you returned safe and sound," Mrs. Gray and Mrs. Meyer said. "It was a mighty risky thing you did."

That was true, Bill Dan reflected as he stretched out in bed. It wasn't long before he fell asleep.

He slept for more than fourteen hours. When he awoke, he found that Darrell had arisen long before the others and had reloaded the horses with the bags of gold ore and taken them to the assayer's office.

Darrell returned while the others were eating the breakfast which Miss Nannie had prepared. He had had a haircut, a shave, and a bath. His fresh clothing made him look like a refined Englishman again, rather than like a prospector tramp. The sight of Darrell's appearance made Bill Dan conscious of his own need for a haircut and a shave.

"The assayer has news for you," Darrell said. "For us, I mean. He estimates — well to tell you the truth, you know the saloonkeeper who sort of acts as banker? You remember — Mr. Collins?"

"Yes," the others nodded. "What about him?"

Darrell's smile broadened. "Well, he said that he would give us sixty thousand dollars for our ore, right off."

Mouths popped open. Bill Dan's fork froze in midair. "Sixty thousand dollars?"

Letitia repeated the amount excitedly.

"Yes. That is, until I acted sort of offish and disinterested. Then he raised it to seventy-five. That's in thousands, too." Finally, he told them that he had sold the ore for eighty thousand dollars.

Eighty thousand dollars! Bill Dan's daze increased when Darrell reminded that he intended to add all of his own money to the general fund. He didn't know just how much it would finally total; perhaps ninety thousand. They need not try to argue it again, he insisted: they were his people, and he would brook no argument. It was worth it to him to have them as his "family" and his friends.

Everyone stopped eating and, after a moment of silence, Bill Dan said, "Six goes into ninety, let's see, six goes into nine one time, and with three to carry, that's three into thirty, I mean six into thirty."

"Fifteen thousand dollars apiece!" Letitia exclaimed breathlessly.

"That's it," announced Darrell, more matter-of-factly. "And I tell you, it's a lot. We didn't find the mine, but we have enjoyed ourselves, and . . . ."

He was interrupted by Roxie Webb, who called back, "Be seein' you all," as he left the table and started off at a trot. His friends laughed, but they didn't need to be told where he was going.

"Thirty thousand dollars," Mrs. Barry murmured to herself for maybe the tenth time. "That's enough to keep me an Letitia the rest of our lives. And we haven't done anything to deserve it."

During the next two hours Bill Dan was busy taking a hot bath, getting a haircut and a shave, having his shoes blacked, and buying new underwear. Then he hurried to Morris' General Store and bought a new suit.

As he approached the adobe home, he felt self-conscious because of the black bow necktie under his white collar. He thought it made him look like a squire.

187

Darrell was alone on the side porch taking his ease despite the chill in the air. When he saw Bill Dan, he rose and stepped toward him with outstretched hand.

Bill Dan shook Darrell's hand in silence, but he couldn't help but wonder. He decided Darrell's gesture was because of his new clothes. Or maybe it was because of their mutual acquisition of wealth. But after all, fifteen thousand did not represent a big fortune. It would be enough, however, to start a business, or buy a ranch with high-grade stock, or invest in a hauling business with teams and wagons. It might even buy a store. And perhaps there would be enough left to build a house and to get married. These details flashed through his mind again, as they had while he was shaving and bathing. But the details had been tinged with anxiety, too. Darrell had his own fifteen thousand, and Letitia had hers. Together, they'd have thirty thousand! And he didn't doubt but what Miss Nannie would join with them in any business. She'd likely live with them, too. His spirits began to hit bottom. His only choice seemed to be to push on to California and . . . .

Darrell interrupted Bill Dan's reverie. "She walked out there in the pasture," he said, gesturing with his head. "She said she wanted to look at Superstition Mountain again in the sunset."

There was a slight pause, then rather foolishly Bill Dan asked, "Who?"

Darrell ignored him and stepped off the porch. "Leonti is downtown," he said. "He seems to want to celebrate on his own. You know, music, dancing, laughing. There'll be lots of girls there. Fine man, Leonti."

188

Bill Dan furrowed his brow. "Sure," he said, "sure thing. Leonti, mighty fine."

Darrell then went on. "I have to admit that I — well, I had hopes for a while. I made plans, or started to. Maybe I was stupid. I didn't do my best. I didn't crowd her. But then there was this thing between you and me. As it turned out, she knew what she was doing all the while. Girls outsmart us, Bill Dan. I figured she had to make up her own mind, and she had already decided to do just that long before I figured to let her." He stopped and looked off.

All Bill Dan could say was, "Uh."

"All right, that's the way it is. Thirty thousand will go twice as far as fifteen thousand. And some day, who knows, you and I and the other fellows just might go back up there to look for that confounded mine again." Darrell smiled at his friend. "People say the Apaches'll be under control by 1900 at the latest. Maybe even by 1895. We'll be crowding forty then, but we could still go if we had a mind to. You and I and Rox and Leonti."

The Englishman suddenly extended his hand, and Bill Dan shook it, meanwhile looking very earnest. He watched in silence while Lord Darrell Duppa, the cultured Englishman, started to walk toward downtown Phoenix.

He stood for about five minutes, staring after his friend, and getting his emotions under control. Presently, in his mind he began to recite ever so formally: *"Miss Letitia, ma'am, you know all about me, but could I maybe possibly hope that you might. . . ."* He let the thought dwindle off because he was scared.

The next moment he squared his shoulders, firmed his lips, and glanced determinedly to the east where Superstition Mountain was turning golden. Then he started to walk with long strides down the little trail to the pasture.

Epilogue

Is there actually a Lost Dutchman Gold Mine? Unquestionably there is.

Most of the characters in this story have been taken from real life, and most of the action is genuine. Lord Darrell Duppa was an English remittance man, who lived in Phoenix and gave the town its name. His picturesque adobe home there still stands and is preserved as a museum.

Countless pioneers migrating west in search of a better life stopped off in Phoenix. Many became excited by the display of gold nuggets by Old Snowbeard the Dutchman and tried to locate the mine.

In the past hundred years, dozens of men have lost their lives in strange disasters while searching for it. Some died by accident, and some by violence. Even today, fortune hunters and curiosity seekers continue to search for it on the rugged slopes of Superstition Mountain.

ABOUT THE AUTHOR

A prolific writer of books and magazine articles, Oren Arnold's favorite subject is the lost mine on Superstition Mountain. Few people had heard of it when he and his wife first came to Arizona, but they proceeded to explore the mountain, and Oren began to research it and write about it. In recognition of his contributions to the literature and folklore of Arizona, the Governor presented him with a plaque for Distinguished Public Service and the City of Phoenix made him its "Man of the Year." Born in Texas and educated at Rice University, Mr. Arnold now divides his residency between a summer home beside the sea in California and a winter home in Phoenix.

ABOUT THE ARTIST

A westerner and a graduate of Arizona State University, Jimmie Ihms has used his versatile artistic talents in films and television, in syndicated newspaper cartoons, and in illustrations for magazines and books. He has taught art at colleges and universities in the Phoenix, Arizona area, where he makes his home with his wife and three children.